a THOUSAND MINUTES
to sunlight

Jen White

FARRAR, STRAUS AND GIROUX

NEW YORK

For Cece

Farrar Straus Giroux Books for Young Readers
An imprint of Macmillan Children's Publishing Group, LLC
120 Broadway, New York, New York 10271

Printed in the United States of America
Designed by Cassie Gonzales
First edition, 2021
1   3   5   7   9   10   8   6   4   2
mackids.com

Library of Congress Cataloging-in-Publication Data

Names: White, Jen, author.
Title: A thousand minutes to sunlight / Jennifer White.
Description: First edition. | New York : Farrar Straus Giroux Books for
Young Readers, 2021. | Audience: Ages 8-12. | Audience: Grades 3-7. |
Summary: To stave off the anxiety plaguing her, Cora counts the minutes
that fill her day and searches for a lost treasure near her home in
California, but the sudden arrival of her long-lost uncle threatens to
upend her carefully-constructed existence.
Identifiers: LCCN 2020015826 | ISBN 9780374300869 (hardcover)
Subjects: CYAC: Anxiety—Fiction. | Buried treasure—Fiction. | Family
life—California—Fiction. | Friendship—Fiction. | Secrets—Fiction.
Classification: LCC PZ7.1.W445 Th 2021 | DDC [Fic]—dc23
LC record available at https://lccn.loc.gov/2020015826

Our books may be purchased in bulk for promotional, educational, or business use.
Please contact your local bookseller or the Macmillan Corporate and
Premium Sales Department at (800) 221-7945 ext. 5442 or by email
at MacmillanSpecialMarkets@macmillan.com.

Do you see that out there?
The strange, unfamiliar light?
It's called the sun. Let's go get us a little.

—Nora Roberts

CHAPTER 1

Saturday: 14 Seconds to Bring in a Dead Guy

When I was born, I didn't breathe for eight minutes. Eight whole minutes. That's four hundred and eighty seconds. Go ahead and try to hold your breath that long. I have and I can't do it.

Dad always says, "That was the longest eight minutes of my life. You scared us to death."

And Mom always says, "Isn't that just like you, Cora? Taking your own sweet time about everything." She says it with a smile.

Dad continues, "The doctor prodded and pushed; he even turned you upside down. He pounded on your little blue back, trying to get you to breathe, but you wouldn't. The clock in the hospital seemed slow—I was convinced it was stuck." He laughs, like he does when he knows he's telling a good story.

"Stuck," Mom says, right on cue. I've heard this story countless times.

"But then you did it," says Dad. "The tiniest cry ever. Not even a cry, just a whimper."

Mom nods like she remembers, but I think, maybe she doesn't. She had an emergency C-section, and the doctors gave her a lot of drugs. Dad says she was out of it. Aunt Janet says Mom took it like a champ—that any normal woman would be out of it because giving birth is bad business. They're twins, Aunt Janet and my mom. They always have each other's backs.

"I was worried, but the doctors said you were normal. No brain damage or anything," Mom always reassures me.

"Not even a little," says Dad. Then he knocks on my head as if he's proving that I'm a healthy kid.

Brain says: I hate this story.

But I'm convinced that somewhere in my cranium, something must have gone wrong.

Brain says: There you go, blaming me again.

Maybe not breathing for eight minutes is what turned my brain from a normal brain to a loud, obnoxious, talking Brain.

I've looked it up on the internet. **Birth Asphyxia: a condition resulting from deprivation of oxygen to a newborn child that lasts long enough to cause harm, usually to the *brain*.**

Brain says: I'm perfectly fine.

Eight minutes without oxygen is a long time and most babies don't survive.

It's enough time for Mom to get bright red and sweaty in her morning workout. Aunt Janet says it's enough time to organize the boutique cash register (which I have done in six minutes) or to wrap a gift. I know it's long enough to make Eggo Waffles for my little sister, Sunshine.

It took less time for Minny, my only friend in the whole

sixth grade—my only friend in my whole, brand-new middle school—to tell me she was moving to Florida. She did it in two minutes and nine seconds, only a week ago. Eight minutes can change your life, just like that.

A silent house, in the middle of the night, might be one of the loneliest places on the planet.

Did you hear that?

Brain says: Absolutely an ax murderer.

Crouched in the hallway, I'm poised for anything. It's 11:31 P.M. to be exact, and a wonder that I can even hear Brain, with my heart hammering in my eardrums.

Inside my head, I count.

1 2 3 4 5

Counting helps. Sometimes counting the minutes is the only thing that soothes the worry that wedges itself on top of my diaphragm. Right now, I'm tucked into a shadow in our long hallway, the one that leads from our bedrooms to our front entry. I adjust my Las Olas Middle School T-shirt that's tucked weirdly into my leggings and pretend I'm brave.

Moments ago, I was perfectly happy, asleep in my room, curled up with Chevy, our bulldog, but I must have heard something.

Brain says: We did.

Chevy now stands at my feet and the hair on the back of his neck bristles. A slight growl gurgles up from the edge of his throat.

A car turns onto our gravel driveway and then there are voices, muted but urgent.

With Chevy at my heels, I creep down the hall to our front door. Something bumps—a soft thud. Shadows waver through the bubbled glass window above our entry. Without warning, the front door flings open with a bang. The handle punches a quick, tidy hole into the wall behind it.

I jump back, but what's weird is that Chevy doesn't bark. Instead, his tail wags.

Dad steps over the threshold, carrying something heavy.

Did he say he was going out? I don't remember.

Then Mom steps into the light. She holds the end part as she and Dad lug a person through our front door.

I hold my breath.

Dad says, "Watch his head."

"*You* watch his head," says Mom. "I'm trying to make sure his filthy shoes don't touch my floors. The cleaners just came today."

The man's face lolls over onto his left shoulder so I can see him more clearly. He's old, like my dad's age.

"Paulo!" whispers Mom to Dad as she lifts the man's legs up even higher. "On the sofa."

My heart bumps.

Dad lifts him up over the coffee table and heads toward our couch. The man's arm flops and almost knocks over one of Mom's conch shells from Hawaii.

"Not that pillow," she says. "The other one, the purple one."

"For goodness' sake," hisses Dad. "Quit worrying about your precious living room." He gently lays the man on the sofa, tossing the pillow—the one with the hand embroidery made by Grandma Altman—safely onto the other couch. Dad's face is strange—like someone has plastic-wrapped it—a frozen expression I don't recognize.

Mom has grown quiet.

The numbers in my head slowly tick off.

64 65 66 67 68

Suddenly Mom is here, waving me away with her hand. "Cora," she says sharply. "What are you doing? Go back to bed."

I have questions, but the silence shushes them.

Mom puts her arm around me and tries to block my view of the strange man. "You're dreaming, sweetie."

Brain says: I don't know about you, but I'm definitely awake.

Her green caftan brushes against her shins. She turns to Dad. "Take her to bed. She doesn't need to see this."

It's only 11:39 P.M., but I've decided that eight minutes is more than enough time for your parents to become people you don't even recognize.

CHAPTER 2

Sunday: 35 Seconds to Inspect a Wall

*I*n my bedroom on San Paulo Street is my favorite place. No schedule. Nothing I have to do. Mom and Dad think it's a great joke that Paulo Altman, my dad, lives on San Paulo Street. Maybe that's why they bought this house when I was five years old.

At five, I'm sure I didn't care about weekends. But now I do, because weekends are like little gifts from the Egyptians who first measured time. Then came the calendar and dividing days into weeks, and weeks into months. Thanks to weekends, I don't *have* to go to school today.

For a moment, I almost forget about last night—the man, about Mom and Dad, and the busted wall—because last night felt like one of those times where your parents are not actually your parents—but instead they're impostors doing very non-parental-type things, like carrying an unmoving person into the house.

Brain says: Aliens.

Brain's been my constant companion since forever. My parents think he's an imaginary friend. Dr. Rosenthal, the psychologist Mom picked out for me a month ago, says I made him up to help with my worries, but he doesn't feel made-up. He feels a part of me.

Brain says: Mind control is very popular in alien culture.

Dr. Rosenthal tries to help me quiet Brain. Sometimes it works, but mostly it doesn't.

I slip out of bed and trip on a jar of coins sitting in the middle of my floor. I have $13.46 in change—if you count the fifty-cent piece (which I do) because it could also be a collector's item. All of it I found with Ruva, the name I gave my metal detector. Dad and I treasure hunt for lost things together at Cat's Cove.

"Dad?" I step out into the hall. The tile floor feels colder than usual. I quietly creep down the hallway, toward the kitchen, and try to prepare myself for the strange man asleep in our living room.

The house sounds empty, but it *feels* empty too—except for Chevy, who chuffs along beside me. His nails click on the tile. He snorts so loudly you can hear him from almost anywhere in the house. The *My Little Pony* theme song blasts from the living room, which means Sunshine is up. Sunshine is obsessed. It's MLP all day, every day, if Mom would let her. Dad says that's what five-year-olds do. They obsess.

"What was I obsessed with when I was her age?" I once asked.

"You don't remember?" asked Dad. "You had a gazillion

wristwatches." Yes, of course. I asked for watches for my birthday that year and a lot of people bought them for me. Their little faces beamed back at me, making a happy *tick-tick-tick*. The spaceship one was my favorite, with a rocket face, red numbers, and a long golden hand that counted down the seconds.

"What does a five-year-old need with all these watches?" Mom would ask, trying to unstrap them from my arms so I could shower. "This just isn't practical, Cora."

I couldn't explain it then, but I can now. Watching those little hands count down—the seconds, the minutes, the hours—made me feel normal. Like there was something else in the world that valued time. Soon, I didn't need the watches to count. I had my own internal stopwatch.

Now I peek beyond the wall into our sitting room, but the sofa is empty. The pillows plumped, like potbellied bulldogs—like Chevy had little purple pillow babies. The sofa sits there innocently, like there was no largish, baby-faced man with stretched-out limbs drooling on it.

Behind me lies the wall where there should be a gaping hole, but it's smooth and whole. The sharp smell of fresh paint attacks my nose. The wall feels tacky. Dad fixed it last night?

"Mom!" I yell into the family room. My voice echoes back—like sonar waves traveling through the ocean. My voice bumps off objects, and then back to me to tell me how far away she is. But it doesn't find her.

"Dad!"

I hold my breath and listen.

"Cora?" Aunt Janet appears beside me.

My cousin, Blue, follows close behind and wraps a chubby arm around my aunt's leg. "When are we leaving? Sunshine's not being nice. I'm bored of *My Little Ponies*."

"We just got here, my love," she says, caressing his cheek.

Aunt Janet and Mom are twins, but they're not identical. Her voice, though. People say the Bell twins sound the same, but I can tell the difference. Mom's voice is slightly deeper, and has bite to it, like an old leather car seat, cracked down the middle by the sun.

"Where's Mom and Dad?" I ask.

Aunt Janet arranges Blue's curly hair. "They had an important appointment they needed to keep. They should be back in a few hours," she says, looking at her wrist that has no watch. She gives Blue's hair another strong pat and then finally meets my eyes.

"There was a guy," I say. "I promise, there was a man lying on the sofa. Last night, on Grandma Altman's cushions . . ."

Aunt Janet looks as if she's trying to decide what to say.

Blue pulls on my pajama pant leg. His eyes are gigantic, brown with green flecks, like mine. "Sunshine's being mean," he says. "Tell her to stop."

I reach down and tie his untied drawstring on his pants. "Okay, buddy. I'm sorry."

Finally, Aunt Janet says, "That's probably a conversation better left to your mom and dad."

"Why?"

She walks toward the family room and calls over her shoulder. "Because."

Brain says: Aliens everywhere.

I check the front window and both cars are gone. They didn't leave together?

Aunt Janet is my favorite aunt. I'm *her* favorite too. She wouldn't hide something from me. We're on the same team. She gets me—all my worries. She talks to Mom for me because Mom takes everything better from Aunt Janet. They were two babies in one belly. For 6,720 hours their hearts beat together as they swam around in the same amniotic fluid. Their heartbeats bumped against one another and said, *It's okay. I'm here. You're not alone.* Sometimes I wish I had a twin who understood me. Someone who had to be my best friend.

Since I said goodbye to Minny just yesterday, now all I have is Sunshine.

Brain says: And me.

Sunshine walks into the kitchen. "Aunt Janet said I can have Cocoa Puffs." She smiles with all her teeth—like she's getting away with something. Mom only lets her have them on her birthday or during the summer or for special occasions.

Aunt Janet's the one who convinced Mom that I didn't have to join Extracurricular Activities. Instead, sometimes I get to work for Mom and Aunt Janet at their children's clothing shop, the Little Boy Blue, or help Dad at his store, Custom Ride. I help Mom and Aunt Janet with inventory, gift wrap, or window displays. That way I'm not forced into what Mom likes to call Social Skills—soccer, acting, or the dreaded swim meet.

Aunt Janet assures Mom that I get plenty of Social Skills helping at the boutique. Which is a relief, because Aunt Janet lets me go into the back room and fold tissue paper if I don't feel like talking to anyone.

Brain says: We've folded tissue paper as high as Mount Everest.

"I saw a guy." I follow Aunt Janet into the den. "I saw him lying on the sofa."

Aunt Janet nods. "You're right. There was a guy, but seriously, Cora. You're going to want to hear this from your parents."

"Is he—um—"

Brain says: Dead. He was absolutely dead. I can tell things like that and that guy was totally, positively, d-e-a-d.

"Was he dead?" I whisper-say.

Aunt Janet says, "Dead? What? No, Cora. He was not dead."

"Then what?"

Her cell phone rings. She looks at it and tells me to go check on Sunshine.

Aunt Janet answers. "I'm here," her voice hushed and concerned. I know it's Mom.

I hold out my hand for the phone because Mom still hasn't returned my texts from this morning, but Aunt Janet shakes her head. So I let Blue lead me to the TV, where he flops on the giant beanbag.

"It's my turn!" he announces.

"Noooo!" Sunshine cries. "It's not fair. This is my house. I get to watch *My Little Ponies* at *my* house." She begins to cry crocodile tears. That's what Dad calls them. Tears that aren't real.

Now Blue starts to cry.

I grab the egg timer sitting next to the TV and spin the dial to eight. "Eight minutes, Sunshine. Blue gets eight minutes to watch what he wants and then it's your turn."

Tears glisten on her cheeks, but she nods. Eight minutes for her, eight minutes for Blue. Sunshine never argues with the egg timer. It's hard to argue with time.

"I don't see why it's your problem," Aunt Janet says into the phone. She stops talking when I stand in front of her. "What, Cora?"

"I'm taking my metal detector down to the beach." I hope she's too distracted to assign me to babysit Blue and Sunshine all day. I need treasure hunting with Ruva, right now.

She frowns a little.

"Are you talking to Mom?"

She grimaces. "You didn't eat."

"I'm not hungry."

She waves her hand. "Fine, you can go for a few hours."

I close my eyes and imagine myself at Cat's Cove, hunting for The Unattainable Find, the heat on my back from the sun. Dr. Rosenthal says I should use visualization when I get worried. I think about Mom and Dad, but all I can see is them bringing in that guy last night. I imagine myself at the cove. But it doesn't make me feel better. Where are Mom and Dad? Who was that man?

I do deep breathing.

It feels like there's a fire and I'm the only one who can smell the smoke.

CHAPTER 3

13 Minutes and 32 Seconds to the Cove

*M*y metal detector, Ruva—the name I call it because of the whirring *roo-vah* sound it makes—hangs on to the back of my bike with two bungee cords. It sticks out like an awkward peacock tail, but without all the beautiful colors. I turn right on Mission and head toward La Quinta Beach. It takes me thirteen minutes to ride my bike to the jetty. I have tried to do it in twelve, but I can't. Last time Minny and I were here, we did it in seventeen.

Minny doesn't care a thing about time and how many minutes things take, like I do.

But we're a good match.

Brain says: Like peas and carrots.

Dad thinks we have a high degree of mutual respect.

Brain says: Or salt and pepper.

Mom thinks it's because we've been friends since second grade.

Brain says: Or how tacos go with Tuesday.

No, Brain, not like Taco Tuesday. It's just because I like her, and she likes me. Our friendship has always been easy. But now that she moved away, I feel lost.

Brain says: You have me.

I pedal faster. Cat's Cove is the only place I want to be. I've got three minutes to beat my time. If the cove is people-free, I'll be fine. Even though it's hot, I zip up my sweatshirt and adjust the hood over my head—down low, to hide my eyes. It's armor. Every glance in my direction bounces off it and hits the person who looks at me.

Pow. Pow. Pow.

I turn right at the corner and maneuver my bike onto the beach path. It's twenty feet wide, usually plenty of space for people and bikes, but today it's packed.

I slow down and dodge a mom pulling a wagon crammed full—a cooler, beach chairs, sand toys, and a playpen, all precariously balanced. A poodle with a mop of hair peeks out from a stroller pushed by a lady. It yips in my direction as I maneuver past the wagon. My heart pounds.

Brain says: Seven people in front of you. Three more behind.

Someone coughs.

I pull my hoodie tighter.

Brain continues to count people as we pass.

Mom says, "Your brain is not a person. Your brain is you."

Dad says, "You are in control, Cora. You have control over everything."

Do I?

Dr. Rosenthal says, "Brain is not real. You are."

I bump a man on my left with the back of Ruva.

"Hey!" he yells. Maybe he just says it, but right now, everything sounds like yelling.

Brain says: The average person can run ten miles per hour.

I pedal faster.

There are about 7.125 billion people on the planet. There are more than 39 million people in California alone. My county, San Diego, has 1.4 million, and 15,000 people live in La Quinta Beach, but that's not counting the tourists. If you count tourists, it might be—a million.

Brain says: Exaggeration doesn't become you.

Aunt Janet says tourists make The Little Boy Blue go 'round. Dad says most customers at his shop, Custom Ride, are lookie-loos, but it's the rich, eccentric ones he loves. They're the people who buy custom cars—vintage originals. Dad's an artist. The cars stand, bright and gleaming in a spotless showroom, preening under the lights, like gigantic Jolly Ranchers, freshly unwrapped. Tourists love Dad's showroom and so do I.

My favorite car in his shop is a vintage convertible VW Bug—bright orange with white leather seats and top. The surf rack, custom created, would lure any beach-loving kook. The trunk's in the front and the engine's in back. Backward, but beautiful.

Sometimes after closing, Dad lets me dry mop the floors, which is the best job because it doesn't require speaking. If I had on my headphones, it would feel just like treasure hunting. I make sure to reach the hard-to-get spots underneath the cars.

I wish every problem could be fixed by a Swiffer with a long-enough handle. I dust until my elbow aches and the floor looks so shiny you would think it fell from the stars.

Dad always says, "Cor-Bell, my customers don't eat off the floors."

Brain thinks Dad's too chipper.

Brain says: I like realists.

Slowly, I pedal my bike past Custom Ride and crane my neck to check the parking lot. Dad's car isn't there. He's never missed a Sunday, until now.

Occasionally, a new wreck will come in that makes Javier, Dad's business partner and friend, groan and shake his head and talk to himself all day. On those days he turns up his music super loud. I love to watch the way a smile spreads across his face when the horn section comes in.

Once, when I was eight, I convinced Dad to let me put a tent up in his back office. I filled it with pillows and blankets and books. But the tent didn't last long.

Mom gave it a disapproving glance. "Take that down. You're in your father's way."

Dad said, "It's fine."

But she made me take it down anyway. Mom tried to soften the blow when she said I could put it up at home. But it wasn't the same. The magic was already lost.

Mom thinks Dad babies me because of my *issues*. At night, their fights are full of my name.

Brain says: And sometimes mine.

Now I pedal faster, away from Custom Ride and toward

Fairfield Park, my least favorite place in La Quinta Beach. The amusement park is a metal-towered, people-infested, noise-violating monstrosity, with sticky walkways and neon lights.

Brain says: Don't look at it.

A long line wraps around Fairfield Park's entrance, protected by a severe-looking King Triton, flanked by two otters that need new paint.

Minny always wanted me to go there with her, and I thought one day I would. But now I can't, since she moved.

The sun beats down on top of my hoodie. I'm baking inside my sweatshirt, but I won't take off my protection.

Brain says: Skin cancer affects 3.3 million people a year in the United States.

I ache for the calm of Cat's Cove.

My tires bump over the train tracks as I follow the sidewalk and jump off the curb and head past the pier.

Brain says: Thirteen minutes.

Waves crash against the jetty as people climb the rocks, laughing and screaming. Water sprays through the air like a gigantic windshield wiper. I continue along the dirt path that dips under Pacific Coast Highway's bridge and duck, even though the road is fifteen feet above me.

I hold my breath. Please don't let anyone be here. It'll ruin everything.

The overpass casts a dark shadow over the entrance of Cat's Cove, but then it opens onto a small lake of quiet water. Waves lap silently as the sun sparkles over the surface, creating miniature prisms of light.

I park my bike.

Water from the harbor flows in on the jetty side, where large patches of black rock creep their way into the cove. Dad says the jetty isn't made of volcanic rock, but of limestone—porous and slick. We've spent hours and hours at the jetty looking for lost things. Treasure hunting is my favorite thing to do with Dad.

It takes me three seconds to realize I'm alone. There's no one here. There's only me.

Brain says: And me.

My chest loosens as I take a deep breath.

Cat's Cove is set at a 90-degree angle and because of the westward ocean current, it turns this place into the drain of La Quinta Beach. Anything dropped, dragged, or tossed into the water will eventually find its way here—the perfect place for hunting treasure.

I slip off my flip-flops and unbungee Ruva. Carefully, I pick my way down to the water, taking care not to stub my toe on the three large rocks that hover near the water's surface. The sand feels like a million glass beads under my feet. The sun warms my back. I want to take off my hoodie.

Brain says: Skin cancer.

The hoodie stays put.

I switch on Ruva and plug my headphones into my metal detector and listen to the comforting beep. Dr. Rosenthal thinks it's because of this methodical sound that hunting treasure is the only place where I can truly think. Everything inside me falls quiet, including Brain.

I have a collection of metal things, and the jar of coins on my closet shelf, but my most important wish is to find the treasure I talk about with Dad almost every day.

The Unattainable Find. Once I find that, everything will change.

CHAPTER 4

9 Minutes Until I'm Reminded That I'm a Weirdo

The sun continues to rise, making the sky look imbalanced. I tilt my head and squint into the glare on the water. It's been a week since Dad and I were last here, and I didn't find anything then—unless you count the rusted tin of breath mints and an old earring, which I don't. I slip my headphones off and check my phone.

This morning, when I found Aunt Janet at my house and no passed-out guy on the sofa, I sent texts to both Mom and Dad. Usually I hate using my cell phone. But this is an emergency. Mom finally texts. It's taken her one hour and twenty-seven minutes to respond.

Mom texts: Be good for Aunt J I'll be home soon Dr. Rosenthal is on call for you, until Dad and I have this mess figured Explain later.

What mess? She still hasn't answered my six questions.

I text Mom again: Where are you? Where's Dad? Who is the passed-out guy? Where is he now?

Why's Aunt Janet here? Why's she acting weird?

I place my phone in my pocket and adjust my headphones back over my hoodie-covered ears. Ruva's monitor stays blank as I swish the paddle a few inches above the sand in a vacuuming motion. The sun continues to bake, but I don't take off my sweatshirt. Dr. Rosenthal says I have a talent for ignoring what I don't want to think about. Instead, I focus on The Unattainable Find—The Cat's treasure.

The legend is this: Catherine Van Larr—known by the nickname "The Cat"—was an eccentric billionaire, the president of a tech company. Twenty-five years ago, a small airplane, which she owned and piloted, crashed into La Quinta Bay. Rescuers found the plane, but no Catherine Van Larr. It was all over the news. The Cat had disappeared. This alone is strange, but people say she may have traveled with a large case of gold coins. Coins she made especially for her, one side stamped with a large *C* and the other with a cat. Because of her, La Quinta Beach is now famous. Treasure hunters come from far and wide to look for her gold. You should see the crowds in the summer. Still, nothing's been found, but Dad and I think it's here.

A few months ago, Minny swore she saw The Cat's gold glinting in the shallows at the jetty, but just when she reached for it, a wave rolled in and it disappeared.

My stomach flips. I believe her—Minny doesn't lie.

Now the water laps at my feet. I swish Ruva back and forth, searching for The Cat's gold. If metal is near, the screen lights up. The faster the beep, the closer I am to what I want. I'm going to find that treasure. I'm going to find it for me and for Dad. But mostly for me. Then I could give Minny enough money so her mom wouldn't have to work, and they could stay in California. I need her.

Brain says: Because of Friday?

Who wants to think about that? I close my eyes and listen for any change in the beeping rhythm.

Beep. Beep. Beep.

Beyond the beeps, I hear something else. Screams. No, laughter—

I pause. My heart races.

Slowly, I turn and inch my headphones above my ears so they pinch my head between the speakers like a headphone halo.

Kids I recognize from school, and some I don't, thread their way under the highway overpass. They slip in between boulders and along the narrow trail. It takes them sixteen seconds until they're on the hill right above me. It's Ando Mendez and his group.

Ando is king of everything.

Okay, maybe not everything, but definitely sixth grade. And if he is king, then the kids around him are his court. They chase one another through the boulders in their cutoff shorts and flip-flops. The girls wear bikini tops—their skin tan, their sun-streaked hair tousled by waves.

Minny knows them.

Ando looks in my direction. His teeth are white and straight against his brown skin, his hair blows in the wind. I can feel his eyes resting on my headphone halo and then on Ruva.

Brain says: Don't make eye contact.

Ando's entourage looks at what he's looking at, and he's looking at me. A girl laughs. Angelica, I think that's her name. "What are you doing?" she yells.

I slip my headphones back over my ears and look at my toes, like they're the most interesting things I've ever seen. Where is Minny when I need her? She would know how to act not-weird.

Ando is a big deal because of his long hair, and his earring, and his dad who used to be a famous surfer. Now his dad sponsors surf tournaments and runs a surf school over near Fairfield Park. Everyone flocks to Bernando Mendez like he *is* the sea.

It takes me five seconds to realize that maybe I'm supposed to say something to them, but I can't think of what.

Brain says: You should run.

I almost do, but then I remember Friday. And how much Mom and Dad want me to be normal. And how I had to have an emergency meeting with expensive Dr. Rosenthal.

Ando stares at Ruva.

Brain says: They know what happened.

I try hard to remember the faces that surrounded me at school on Friday, but I can't.

"WEIRDO," someone says.

It takes zero seconds for everyone to laugh. Even Ando does.

But they're right. I am a weirdo. Heat creeps up my neck and into my face. It's getting hotter in the hoodie, but I don't take it off.

"Who's that?" asks a girl with a French braid down to her waist and a seaweed bracelet on her arm. I don't remember her name, but I want to tell her that sometimes I make bracelets out of seaweed too, for Sunshine.

The hill is covered with ice plants, yuccas, aloe vera, and boulders. A large mass of aloe vera plants, as tall as two men, shivers. Something rustles behind it. Everyone turns to look.

"Who's there?" asks Angelica.

No one answers.

"Let's go," says Ando. He climbs up the embankment, his group following close behind. In two seconds, they disappear over the hill. And even though I want Ando and his friends gone, I realize I'm left alone with a rustling plant.

"Helloooo," says a boy's voice. It vibrates down the slope and right into my eardrums.

I almost say something.

Mom would have yelled hi. Dad would have asked, "Who's there?" Minny would have laughed.

But me?

Brain says: You shouldn't talk to plants.

I step back and just as I'm about to use my outside voice, my headphones blow up with noise—rapid-fire beeps, one after another. Ruva's screen glows.

I look down at the sand. Something is here.

Kneeling quickly, I jam my hand into the wet grit, hoping that the *something* is near the top. Sand crabs claw against my wrists, and I could grab them if I want. I could grab a huge, hulking mess of them and take them home to Sunshine.

Brain says: Don't get distracted.

I unhook the sifter from my belt loop and shovel through great gobs of sand. My fingers barely brush the surface of something hard. Metal?

Brain says: The Unattainable Find.

Brain won't admit it, but he loves treasure even more than I do.

I dig as deep as I can, willing my arms to be longer, but something thuds down the hill behind me. I turn. A boulder, about the size of a watermelon, rolls and then skids to a stop as it reaches the foot of the embankment.

"Hey!" A boy slides down after it, wearing long sleeves and goggles. A weird metal crown balances on the top of his head; thorns cling to his clothes.

In one giant motion I yank my hand out of the ground. Sand and seawater drip down my arm as the beeping continues.

He bounds toward me like a grasshopper—the goggles distort his eyes and the crown resembles antennae. "Nice! Whatcha find?" he asks.

I squint. Does he go to my school?

Brain says: There's a whole space station on that weirdo's head.

Scrambling up, I take a few steps back, my hand still gripping Ruva.

"Do you have a permit for that thing?"

He's joking, I think. Also, I don't like jokes.

My stomach tightens as the lost thing slowly melts into sand oblivion. The hole's filled back in with silt and water. I can't lose it, the thing I almost got. The thing I would have gotten if this kid hadn't bothered me. I try to memorize where I am standing, maybe twenty-five paces from the bottom of the hill. There's a large yucca plant with an orange flower to the left of me.

The kid comes closer. He lifts his goggles and smiles. "I just want to look." He reaches for Ruva.

"No." I pull my metal detector away.

A wave comes up and erases the last signs of my hole.

I bolt to my bike. My fingers fumble as I secure Ruva with bungee cords and throw my leg over the bicycle seat, slamming my feet onto the pedals. My gears creak like rusted hinges as I pump my legs. The bike wobbles. Ruva isn't lashed on properly.

"Stop!" Aloe Vera Kid yells from behind.

But I would never.

On Pacific Coast Highway a car honks. I pump my legs harder until I reach the street. PCH is filled with traffic. I glance over my shoulder and even though I'm safe, the I'm-being-chased feeling stays.

My fingers twitch. I know I felt metal. I pause, surrounded

by exhaust and thunder in my chest. I almost turn back, but then, I don't.

Stupid Aloe Vera Kid.

I'll go back when no one's there. If Dad's home, he'll want to come too. I've waited this long.

Brain says: And now you get to wait longer.

CHAPTER 5

4 Minutes and 1 Second Until I Am Humiliated

I pedal fast toward home.

A water bottle bounces past my front tire and into the gutter. Wetness seeps through my hoodie and onto my back. Someone yells, "You suck!" from a passing car. Cackles surround me, mixed with car fumes.

There are seven billion people in the world. Yes, that's six billion, nine hundred ninety-nine million, nine hundred ninety-nine thousand, nine hundred ninety-three too many.

Brain says: Lucky for you, you still have me.

I pedal and blink hard—tears leak from my eyes, filling my earhole with water. I try to catch my breath. The sidewalk looks fuzzy.

Brain says: Not again.

"Cora! Cora Altman." Two shapes waver ahead of me. I squeeze my eyes closed and when I open them again, they're not floating shapes anymore, but real people.

It takes me three point five seconds to recognize Mr. Farns, my social studies teacher, who I've known for thirty-four school days, since middle school began—Dad knows him too.

I get off my bike and try to make my face look normal, but how can I when Brain won't shut up?

"How are you?" Mr. Farns asks. I take a deep breath like Dr. Rosenthal says I should. Breathing is directly related to my *not* having a panic attack. That and paying attention to my surroundings.

Dad will expect me to be friendly.

Mr. Farns's eyebrows crinkle together. I think he's trying to look sympathetic, but the sweat marks under his arms are distracting. "This is my wife, Evangeline."

"Hello," she says. She holds a plastic bag full of Kentucky Fried Chicken, gripping it close to her body with both hands.

"Cora's in my first-period social studies class."

Evangeline nods, the bag slipping from her grasp.

Dr. Rosenthal says I need to notice body language and facial expressions because communication is like a treasure hunt.

I wonder if Evangeline's shirt has sweat marks too. What if *I* have sweat marks? I tuck my hands under my armpits.

"Are you feeling better?" he asks.

My heart pounds.

Brain says: Friday is dead to us.

I make my head nod.

"That's good," says Mr. Farns. "Will you be in class tomorrow?" I nod.

"What's that? A metal detector?" he asks, looking at Ruva.

"Evangeline, what do you think of that?" He chuckles to himself. Mr. Farns reaches a stubby finger toward Ruva.

I inch it away.

"How's your dad?"

Mr. Farns taught Dad in sixth grade. That's how old he is. He's ancient. "Tell him I've got a car I'd like him to look at. My son's—the gears keep slipping."

Dad does a lot of car-favors for people he knows, and that includes Mr. Farns.

"If there's anything you need, you just let me know. Even if you just want to talk," he says.

Brain laughs.

I would laugh out loud too, if I did that sort of thing in public. A car horn blares.

Evangeline says, "So nice to meet you, Cora." They pass me and continue across the highway toward the beach.

Brain says: Good riddance.

CHAPTER 6

12 Minutes and 2 Seconds Until Aunt Janet Jogs My Memory

When I get home, Dad's car still isn't in the driveway and neither is Mom's.

I park my bike, stash Ruva in the garage, and go silently through the door that leads from the garage to the kitchen. I slink down the hallway into my bedroom. My bed is a perfect cocoon of blankets. So cozy that I dive right in—my shoes still on.

Chevy gallops in on his tiny legs; his collar jingles. You can't help but feel a little bit better when you hear the cheery clink of a dog collar. I heave him onto my bed and breathe in his doggy smell.

"Hey, boy." I scratch behind his ears. "How was today with Aunt Janet and Sunshine?"

His tail wags. Dogs are so much better than people. Easier to understand too. Happy? Wag your tail. Unhappy? Growl. Easy peasy.

My treasures sit on my dresser—a Matchbox car, an old lighter covered with flowers and vines, a tiny mirror, a ring of brass, and a lipstick case. Five items that now have a home with me.

Brain says: You lost number six.

The weight of the lost thing sits cold in my hand. I can almost feel it, slick with sea moss—sticky with salt.

The day drags on and on until I hear Aunt Janet yell my name from down the hall. Chevy licks my face as I lie in my bed and stare at the ceiling.

"When did you get home?" She stands in my doorway, hands on her hips, her mouth a thin line.

I say louder than I mean to, "A while ago."

Chevy scoots off my bed and plows into the dirty laundry sitting on my floor. He loves to sit in piles of things.

Aunt Janet runs her hands through her short hair. Her earrings—metallic wires—sway as she tries to catch my eye. "Didn't you see my texts?"

"No."

"*People* use cell phones. *You* can use a cell phone. I wouldn't have let you go if I knew you wouldn't respond."

Brain says: Cell phones give you brain tumors the size of pineapples.

"I'm sorry," I say. "I got distracted." I know. *I know.* I'm not making it easy for her.

"It's been a weird day."

Aunt Janet flings her gigantic purse over her shoulder and almost knocks the treasures off my dresser. She looks at her watch. "I've got to go. Blue is whiny and I have sidewalk sale prep."

"The sale is tomorrow?" I ask as I stand in front of my dresser to protect my things. I love getting ready for a sale. I can make a tag in twelve seconds.

"Next week, but you need to stay here with Sunshine. Your dad is supposed to be home pretty soon. But I cannot, in good conscience, leave you unless you *promise* to keep your cell phone on and promise to answer it. Okay? I'm only five minutes away."

"But I'm good at the tags . . . ," I say.

She nods. "Yes, you are. You're the best, Cora. But right now, you need to hold down the fort."

Hold down the fort is an idiom; I learned about them in English class. But Aunt Janet and Mom seem to be the only people who use them. In Mom's family, everyone should soldier through and fight tooth and nail. They are trying to make me into a good, stiff-upper-lip, holding-down-the-fort little soldier.

"Where are Mom and Dad?"

She fakes a cheery voice. "I promise they'll explain everything when they get home."

"*You* tell me." And I must look extra pathetic, because Aunt Janet finally sits on my bed. Her purse clunks to the floor like she's carrying rocks. She must have Blue's Hot Wheels collection inside.

"I guess it's okay. You'll find out soon enough. Your dad—"

Just then Blue bursts through my bedroom doorway, crying. "Sunshine says she's queen of everything and is in charge of the egg timer. She's still watching stupid pony shows and I WANT TO GO HOME!"

CHAPTER 7

1 Hour and 47 Minutes Until I Understand Everything, Sort Of

It takes Aunt Janet thirty-seven seconds to leave our house with a crying Blue behind her.

Brain says: Good riddance.

I make SpaghettiOs for Sunshine from a can. She likes to eat it cold, with a spoon. Mom won't let her eat straight from the can when she's home. I will. And sometimes Dad does too.

"Can I have another?" she asks. Her lips are rimmed with a weird orangish red.

Brain says: Whatever you say, that is not real pasta sauce.

"Finish that and then maybe."

My phone sits on the edge of the counter. Brain and I have come to a compromise. It's turned on *and* I plan to answer it if it rings—if I don't hold it up to my head. Texting or speakerphone only.

The phone beeps.

I pick it up.

Dad has finally responded to my twelve texts.

He texts: Be home soon. Call Aunt Janet if you
need anything.

That's it?

What about: Sorry about the weird guy we dragged into
the house last night. Or, sorry your mom and I have been gone
all day. I'll explain everything immediately. I check my text I
sent to Minny last night. She still hasn't texted me back.

I texted: I miss you!!!!!!!!

It stares blankly at me, waiting for her response.

Brain says: Why'd you use so many exclamation points?

I like exclamation points. I feel like I'm using my outside
voice in a text, which I never use in my real life. Minny's probably busy unpacking or building IKEA shelves or arranging
her room.

Brain says: Or making new friends.

Already?

"Is that Mommy?" asks Sunshine.

"No."

"I want to talk to Mommy." She reaches for my phone.

I hand it to her. "But don't put it up to your ear."

Her forehead wrinkles.

Brain says: Pineapple tumors.

"Just use the landline."

"I did. I left a message when Aunt Janet was here." Her
eyes fill with tears. "When are Mom and Dad coming home?"

"Soon," I say, even though nothing is certain, and nothing
feels right. Mom and Dad aren't responding to Sunshine? It's
all strange.

After her can of SpaghettiOs, Sunshine and I watch *My Little Pony's Merry Christmas Parade*, even though Christmas is months away. Then we play Ice Cream Scoops of Fun three times and I let her win twice.

Brain says: That's two times too many.

Then we feed Chevy and I fold all the towels in the dryer and Sunshine helps by watching me do everything. After that, it's getting dark—even though it's only seven o'clock—and I have her put on her MLP pajamas and then I read to her.

I read to her for sixteen minutes and three seconds. We read *Miss Nelson Is Missing!* Sunshine asks questions about Miss Viola Swamp. And if Viola Swamp and Miss Nelson are the same person. And why is there a black wig in Miss Nelson's closet?

Brain says: This story is so obvious.

But I answer all her questions very patiently, like a good big sister. And finally, I tell her yes, Miss Nelson and Viola Swamp are the same person. I don't want her to have bad dreams about some scary substitute teacher who will come to kindergarten and terrorize her. Little girls with names like Sunshine should have only nice stories and good dreams.

I like to take care of her, even if she is Mom's favorite.

Brain says: She's not mine.

"Thank you, Cora." Sunshine wraps her arms around my neck, smelling slightly of SpaghettiOs. The hug is the best part of reading to her. Normally, I don't like to be hugged, but with Sunshine, it's okay. It lasts for sixteen seconds and I don't pull away. I wait until she stops hugging me, because that's what you're supposed to do with little kids. She can't help that she is everything Mom wants in a girl. If I were Mom, Sunshine would be my favorite too.

I close Sunshine's door and walk down the hallway into my bedroom. It's too quiet.

I pick up my cell. No one has texted me, except Aunt Janet. Not even Minny.

Brain says: Tumors the size of pineapples.

I know. I know.

My fingers fumble.

I text Aunt Janet: Everything's ok. Have you heard from Mom?

Minny would laugh at me. She says texts don't have to be full sentences, but that doesn't feel right.

Aunt Janet texts: Good job Cora thnks for txting someone will b home soon

Darn Blue and his meltdowns. What was she going to tell me?

Brain says: What if that guy comes back tonight?

But he can't, can he?

I try to distract Brain by calculating the number of hours to fly from California to Florida, where Minny is. Does she like it? Does her new bedroom have wallpaper with purple llamas like her old room? Does her mom still let her have ice cream for breakfast on Fridays? Florida is three hours ahead of California. She might be asleep. I text her anyway.

I text: Mom and Dad are gone.

I text: There was a passed-out, not-dead guy on our sofa.

I text: I almost found something at Cat's Cove.

I text: Why don't you text me back?

My heart bumps.

I imagine Cat's Cove at dusk—how everything turns pink and gold when the sun goes down. The soft lap of waves against the shore. The lost thing floating like a star, suspended underneath the sand.

Forty-seven seconds pass.

My phone buzzes.

Minny texts: In bed tlk tmrw

Minny has cousins and a grandma in Florida, but does she really love it already? Doesn't she miss me? My stomach churns with SpaghettiOs.

I text: Talk now?

Brain says: Tumors.

Without waiting for her response, I call her. It rings twice and then she answers.

"Cora?" Her voice is full of sleep.

"It's me," I say, relieved. I do have a friend, even if she's 2,632 miles away.

If Brain had eyes, he'd be rolling them.

"Are you okay?"

"Yes."

"I thought you hated your cell phone," she whispers.

"I do."

"I'm not supposed to have my phone after nine. Mom forgot to take it."

I nod and then remember she can't see me.

"Okay." I finally gulp, my throat strangled.

"I'll call you tomorrow. I have to go. I don't want to wake up Mom," she whispers, and then hangs up before I can say goodbye.

She sounded tired but good. We're still friends.

Brain says: Long-distance friendships are the worst.

Before she left, Minny gave me her flight information. The flight was supposed to be five hours and two minutes, but it actually took four hours and forty-one minutes because of a jet stream. And just when I begin to feel better thinking about time differences and jet streams—

Brain says: Did you hear that?

CHAPTER 8

16 Minutes Until an Intruder

*I*f I could turn invisible, I would. There is a sound—a thud outside my bedroom door.

Brain says: There it is again.

I wrap my comforter around me and shrink into the covers. Even I can't deny the bedroom door creaking ever so slightly—in seconds the air feels all sucked up. My heartbeat bumps into my eyeballs.

A wet black nose pushes through and the door swings open.

"Chevy!" I say, and instantly feel ridiculous. He probably fell asleep in the laundry room in the pile of clean clothes. Poor bulldogs, they can never breathe properly. He snorts and snuffles and goes right over to my trash can to look for anything good to chew.

"Hey, boy," I say, rubbing his sides. I feel much better with him here. Chevy isn't a guard dog, but he would bark if something was wrong.

I feed him a bit of crust from yesterday's sandwich left on my dresser.

Chevy snorts and smiles up at me.

"You're a good boy, aren't you?" I say. He wags his tail so hard it makes him fall over and he's so lazy—he just stays there.

I lug him onto my bed. He snuffles under my comforter, grunting like a pig with allergies. Small spaces make me feel better too. Dad says that when I was little, my preschool teacher would always find me in the large cabinet underneath the sink. I breathe in the memory of dark quiet, hidden behind gingham curtains.

Mom hated my under-the-sink-kind-of-weirdness. "Cora," she'd say. "Stand up straight. You're not an animal, sweetie."

Brain says: Actually, we are.

I really try to make Mom happy. But she knows I'm not normal.

Chevy sniffs in the direction of my dresser, but the sandwich is gone.

"Come on, boy," I say. But he's not completely convinced he wants to get out of the cozy nest I've made for us.

I stand. "Let's get food!"

He jumps off the bed, his tail wagging like it might helicopter him into outer space.

We go down the hall and examine the entry wall again. Chevy sniffs it. The paint is dry, but a little bumpy over the patch.

He whines.

I pull a cheese stick out of the fridge and give him half,

which he swallows in one gulp. I stare out the kitchen window as streetlights splash white across our pebbled driveway. Dad's restored VW Bus that he barely drives sits like it's waiting for something—stalled, just like today.

Brain says: Like you.

I turn and slide down against the kitchen cabinets, encircling my arms around my legs, making myself into a hermit-crab ball.

Chevy puts his head on my lap and begs for more cheese.

Headlights flash across the kitchen cabinets. Gravel crunches as a car pulls into our driveway. Finally—Mom or Dad.

Chevy lifts his head—his ears perk up. He gives a short, gruff bark, lodged at the back of his throat.

I stand and see Dad through the window. He walks up the path, but then stops and stares at the sky. His hair stirs in the breeze and his shoulders slump like he's holding something heavy only he can see. Forty-five seconds and then Dad walks into our house.

We reach the front door at the same time.

"Hey," I say.

Dad's mouth smiles, but not his eyes. He clears his throat. "Cor-Bell. It feels like a hundred years. I've missed you." He squeezes the back of my neck with his fingers and then gives me a hug, his solid arms warm around my shoulders. *See. Everything's okay. I don't have to worry.*

"Where's Mom?" I ask when he sets me free.

"Aunt Janet's."

"It's Sisters' Weekend?"

He shifts his weight. "Something like that. Don't worry, Cora baby."

And maybe it's the way he says *baby*, but I swallow the question sitting in my throat. The one that asks: What's wrong?

Dad drops his keys on the tile floor. We both flinch. The clatter bounces off every flat surface, disturbing the quiet that fills the house.

Finally, he looks at me. "What have you been up to all day?"

"Nothing, but . . ." I remember the hole in the wall, and the man on the couch, and Mom's angry face.

"How was Sunshine?" he asks.

I follow him past the entry and into the kitchen. He flips on the light and opens the fridge. He stares into it, then closes the door.

"Fine," I say. "You know, she's Sunshine."

Dad laughs, which makes me feel a little better. Things can't be completely awful if Dad can still laugh. "You want to know what's going on?"

Brain says: Of course, dummy.

I nod. My stomach feels so tight, like I can turn into a hermit crab again.

"Did you manage to get Sunshine in bed?" he asks.

I nod. I *can* do things. I *can* help.

He grabs the milk out of the fridge and a box of Froot Loops from the pantry. "You know the story of The Cat?"

Of course. The billionaire Catherine Van Larr. The plane crash. The Unattainable Find.

It takes him twenty-one seconds to pour his cereal. "I found something that was lost." His voice cracks.

My heart bumps. "The Unattainable Find?" I ask. I feel light-headed. Then jealous. Then angry. We were supposed to find it together.

"Better," he says, his eyes watery.

What could be better than The Cat's treasure?

"That man you saw last night?"

I nod.

"He's my brother."

"Uncle Joaquin?" He lives in Texas and we don't get to see him very often.

"No, the other one."

I am silent. The other one?

Brain says: Did he just make up a brother?

Dad says, "My other brother. Remember? I told you."

I pause, then nod. The one who ran away. The one I've never met. The one Grandma Vo never talked about.

Dad rubs his eyes, hard. "We haven't heard from him in years." He stuffs a huge spoonful of cereal into his mouth and finishes chewing. "When he left, I was twelve, he was seventeen. He used to take me surfing, he loved cars—he had an old Land Cruiser. Vo, Uncle Joaquin, and I thought he might have died." His voice fades.

Brain says: I knew there was a dead guy.

"He has problems—he drinks too much alcohol. But last night he called me and said he was here, at La Quinta Beach. He wanted to see us—me." Dad's voice catches. "He said he's

46

ready to get help. So I'm helping him. He's in detox right now, then he'll go to that new rehabilitation center they built down by the pier."

He rubs his face. "You know what rehab is, right?"

I nod. Where people go to have doctors help them get all the drugs and alcohol out of their system. Minny's dad had to do that.

"Your mom isn't very happy that I'm letting him come around again or that I'm helping him at all. That's why she's at Aunt Janet's right now." He runs his hand through his hair. It stands up like a rooster tail. "Don't worry, she'll calm down."

I nod again, like I understand. But there are too many questions. How long will he be in detox and rehabilitation? Where will he live when he gets out? Why is Mom mad? My stomach squeezes into a hard ball.

Dad accidentally knocks over the cereal box and little O's roll off the counter like the questions bouncing in my brain. A blue one lands on my bare foot. Dad's lost brother was on our sofa last night? Dad's lost older brother with a roundish baby face and *addictions*?

In eight seconds, I realize, dead people can come back to life.

CHAPTER 9

Monday: 37 Minutes Until I Am Forced to Do Something I Hate

This morning Mom's still at Aunt Janet's. Dad's in the garage talking on the phone about the lost-brother-who-Mom-hates-and-who-drinks-too-much, and he has hardly looked at me, so how can I tell him about The Unattainable Find I may have found at Cat's Cove?

Brain says: The almost treasure.

Fine. The *almost* treasure, the one suspended in sand. My fingers itch for Ruva. If only I can stay home and sneak out to find it.

"Dad," I say, standing in the doorway of the garage. His head disappears behind a stack of cabinets. He waves me away.

Sigh.

So that leaves me to make cereal for Sunshine and to get us ready for school.

SCHOOL.

Because of Friday, it's the last place I want to be, especially now that Minny isn't here to save me.

Brain says: Today is very bad.

Brain has a headache. With each pulse, my head throbs.

Sunshine drinks the milk from her Cocoa Puffs and leaves a chocolate mustache above her lip. This is her second bowl.

"You're going to make yourself sick."

She shakes her head. "I want more."

I can't help but be distracted by Dad. His talking sounds like *hum-hum-hah-hum*. And then there's the constant banging of metal things. What's he looking for?

Sunshine lies across the kitchen island, too close to me. The chocolaty milk mustache shimmers above her lip and makes my stomach twist over on top of itself.

Brain says: I might throw up.

Sunshine jumps off the counter and stomps her foot dangerously close to mine. "Cora, now tie my shoes."

I slide down the kitchen cabinets and sit on the cold tile. My big toe's on top of the chipped piece in the shape of Australia. The lights are so bright. Someone has added extra bulbs to the ceiling. If I concentrate very hard, I can almost see luminous bulbs wave in front of my eyelids. I close my eyes.

Luminous. Mom likes that word.

When my baby sister was born at 4:11 A.M. on May 16, Mom says she was luminous. That's why they named her Sunshine, because she filled the hospital room with light—at least that's what I imagine. Maybe Sunshine's atoms released light photons (that's what happens when electrons get excited). My sister's very enthusiastic.

Brain says: That is scientifically unsound.

When she was born, I was seven years old. I stayed with Aunt Janet for three days and when I came home, baby Sunshine cried all day and night. She never quit. She was like a tiny, sweaty, screaming machine. When she stopped it was only to take a breath, so she could cry harder.

Mom says I remember it wrong. Sunshine was an angel baby. Sunshine was heaven.

So maybe I can't remember everything, but I do know she made my parents very happy, because after they had me, they'd been trying to have a baby for a long time. She is their sunshine.

Brain says: Then you are the night.

Now Sunshine crouches down, her face inches from mine. I feel her, even though I haven't opened my eyes yet.

She whispers her chocolaty breath in my face. "Cora, tie my shoes, puleeeezzze."

"Okay." I turn my face away.

I take three giant breaths and open my eyes. "Count with me, Sunshine."

She shakes her head. "Why do you always want me to count with you?"

So, I count in my head.

Breathe. Count. Breathe. Count.

For the last month, Dr. Rosenthal has said it's important to have strategies that help me feel better when I'm anxious. But lately the things that used to work, like counting and breathing and paying attention to my surroundings to distract Brain, don't. Mom really likes Dr. Rosenthal. She says she's the best.

Brain says: She's not.

Sunshine taps her shoes on Australia.

I grab her frayed laces. "When are you going to learn to tie your own shoes?" I wrench them into little bows and double knots. It takes me twenty-two seconds.

She shrugs. "Daddy does it."

"But what happens when you're at school? Who ties them then?"

"They don't come untied at school."

"But what if they do?"

"They don't."

Dad walks into the kitchen with his phone still attached to his ear.

Brain says: Pineapple-sized tumors.

"Dad." I wave my arm to get his attention. But he barely glances at me as he walks down the hall to his and Mom's bedroom.

Sunshine zips her *My Little Pony* lunch box into her backpack and then swings it two times around the kitchen. The third time it hits me on the head. My head throbs with school worry, and Mom and Dad worry, and no Minny worry, and too bright kitchen light bulbs.

I close my eyes.

Sunshine whispers in my ear, "We still have to do affirmations."

"No. Mom's not here."

Metal grates across the tile counter and I know Sunshine has the box. I open my eyes. She kneels on the kitchen counter and goes through the metal recipe box that holds Mom's affirmations.

"You can't stand on the counter," I say.

"I'm not standing. I'm sitting and Daddy doesn't care."

I hate affirmations. I know they're only for me. Mom thinks I have a mind-over-matter thing. A brain thing.

Brain says: I'm the problem?

Mom says a positive attitude is the key to success. Affirmations are supposed to change me.

Sunshine pulls out a card and holds it up. "Here," she says. "Read it."

I shake my head.

"Cora," says Sunshine.

"Get off the counter."

"Dad doesn't care if I'm on the counter!" Her voice shakes and her eyes fill with tears. The dirty white affirmation notecard begins to crumple under the weight of her clenched fist.

"Fine." I hold out my hand. "I'll read it. But he does too care."

Sunshine smiles and it's like the tears were never there.

"What don't I care about?" Dad calls from the hallway.

This is my chance. I take a deep breath. "Dad, I can't go to school."

He stops in the kitchen with his hands on his hips.

Sunshine begins, "I can sit on the counter, right, Daddy?"

Dad doesn't reply to either of us. "I forgot to look one more place." He disappears back into the garage from the kitchen.

I turn the affirmation card over. In Mom's handwriting it says, *I have lots of friends who love me.* I swallow hard.

Brain says: Nope.

"Read it." Sunshine stands on her tiptoes. "It's in cursive. Cursive's hard."

I swallow. "Sunshine has lots of friends who love her."

Her smile is immediate. "I do," she says shyly. "Now say, Sunshine *and* Cora have lots of friends who love them."

Dad walks back through the kitchen, for the first time without his phone to his ear. "Let's go, ladies. Look at the clock. School's a-calling."

"Yay!" Sunshine grabs her backpack, opens the front door, and runs out.

Finally, he really looks at me—his hand clenched around his phone like a talon.

I lie on the kitchen floor with my arm flung over my eyes. I peek at him through the thin crack between my arm and my face.

"Come on, Cora." Dad squats near my right foot. He thumps the bottom of my shoe. "You can do it."

Brain says: It's a bad day.

"Cora, I need to get to work."

Slowly, I pull myself up to sitting. I never noticed the dark circles under Dad's eyes until now. Has he always had them?

"I'm old enough to stay home by myself. And, Dad, there's a treasure. I think I found something at Cat's Cove." I just need one day without Mom here, without her willing me to be a happy, chipper, ready-to-conquer-the-world little soldier.

Plus, there's no Minny at school to meet me.

I look at my watch. It is 11:08 A.M. in Florida. Does Minny even miss me at her new school? Today's our first day without each other.

Dad takes a deep breath. I can see him thinking, weighing, deliberating—all of it across his forehead, creased with three large lines.

"Cora, I'm sorry. But today, you're just going to have to face it. If you're feeling well enough to want to treasure hunt, then you're well enough to go to school." He thinks I'll go down to the cove without Mom here to keep an eye on me.

"But Dr. Rosenthal said—"

"Dr. Rosenthal says the sooner you get back to your normal routine, the better it will be for you."

Brain says: He sounds like Mom. That is not a compliment.

A tear leaks out of my eye. Just one.

Brain says: Crying is for babies.

Tears are just the body's response to stress. I read about it on WebMD. I quickly wipe it away.

"Get in the car, please. Your mother will throw a fit if I let you stay home again. There's no negotiating."

I drag myself to standing. It takes eighteen seconds.

Dad's eyebrows unknot. "You'll see, Cor-Bell. It won't be so bad." He follows Sunshine out the front door.

I grab my backpack from the kitchen island. It weighs one thousand pounds.

Brain says: That's inaccurate.

Sixth grade makes everything feel so heavy.

Before school started, Mom said, "Give it two months, Cora. You'll see, in two months, you'll love it." I've given it one month and twelve days. Middle school makes me feel like I've lost my protons *and* my electrons. One by one, atoms seep from my skin and leave me a walking, counting Cora-shell.

My mother forgets who I am.

There's no one in the whole school who'll be happy to see me.

Brain says: You have me.

Dad says, "Cor, let's take the van!"

I text Minny: `Do you like your new school?`

She doesn't respond.

CHAPTER 10

8 Minutes and 47 Seconds Until I Know More about Uncle #2

*F*renzied. That's Las Olas Middle School.

Students run, cars honk, doors slam, but Dad and I sit parked in front of the school with Dad on his phone, oblivious. Nine minutes ago, we dropped off Sunshine with her *My Little Pony* backpack, her lost-tooth smile, and a bounce in her step. Mom calls it gumption. Dad calls it self-esteem.

Brain says: We'll see how long that lasts.

I look out the window. The backpacks of the students look so very light as they sprint down the sidewalks—trying to beat the tardy bell. They rush across the grass, past The Great Wave—our school's mascot. It's a large blue-and-white plaster wave towering over the front lawn. I'm trying *not* to beat the bell. Tardies don't scare me. Lateness does not strike fear. It's the people inside the school who do.

Now that Minny's gone, I have no one. She's been kidnapped by a mother who has a new job and the Wizarding

World of Harry Potter and Disney World (which I don't care about because of the crowds), and her grandma and cousins. Before she left, Minny was excited about Florida, even though she said she'd miss all her friends, especially me.

Dad usually understands the heaviness of it all, but not today. Today he's distracted, and I know why. The lost older brother. I dislike him already; Mom and I can agree on that. When will she come home from Aunt Janet's?

Dad rolls down the window and the ocean breeze ruffles our hair. Don't think I don't know what he's trying to do. I love the VW Bus. It's a peace offering, sort of.

The van has two bench seats in the back and a flowered curtain you can pull across in the middle for privacy. The bench seats fold down and make one large bed, and the top pops up like a spyglass, giving the van added windows. It is perfect and orange and smells like an old rubber band. It's like traveling in a lost treasure.

Everyone in my family agrees that middle school is H-E-double hockey sticks. Even Aunt Janet says Mom hated it and cried every school day her first month of sixth grade. That's nineteen crying days. Mom says Aunt Janet remembers it wrong, but Aunt Janet remembers everything.

The tardy bell blares throughout the school and I expect it to shatter every surface it touches, but it only shatters me. Not Dad. Not the VW van. Not Brain. Only me. Sound travels fast—762 miles per hour, to be exact.

Brain says: Neurons are faster than sound.

I know, Brain.

Brain's very competitive—the average brain neuron fires two hundred times a second.

As the seconds click by, it's hard not to think about the treasure. What if, yesterday, it was The Unattainable Find? If I found it, I wouldn't *only* be the sixth-grade weirdo who has panic attacks. I'd be special. Dad would be proud. Mom would love for me to get recognized for something extraordinary. Minny would have to come back to celebrate. Everyone at school would know that I'm the girl who found Catherine Van Larr's treasure. The warmth of the daydream washes over me.

Dad answers another call. Maybe I can sneak into the back of the van, close the flowered curtains, and sleep in the parking lot of Custom Ride while he's at work.

"Yes," Dad says into the phone.

There is a twelve-second pause.

"No. No. He doesn't have my consent." Dad looks at me and says abruptly, "I'll have to call you back." He pats my arm, trying to pretend he's not thinking about Uncle #2. "What'd you want to tell me, Cor-Bell? You found the treasure?"

I shake my head. Suddenly it feels wrong to talk about the treasure when I can tell Dad's so worried.

He gestures out the window at The Great Wave. "When I went to this school, I used to sit under that wave and wonder about my big brother, about where he went, and why he hadn't come home. I hoped he was safe."

I wait.

"Now, I have to take care of him. He's supposed to be out of detox in three days and then he'll start an in-patient rehab for a few months. The first three days are crucial."

"After that, is he going to live with us?"

"I'm not sure. Mom wouldn't like me talking about this with you. I'll answer all your questions, but—" He looks at his phone. "I've got to go and so do you." He turns on the ignition.

Four students run past the front office, hoping, I'm sure, not to run into Dr. Shurtzer, the principal, because she's mean—at least that's what Minny says. That's what everyone says.

Dad's cell phone buzzes, again.

"Dad, I can't do it."

"Cora, make my life a little easier and *go to school*. Please," he begs. "It could be the beginning of new friendships for you."

"Or the end," I whisper-say.

I open the door and lug my thousand-pound backpack over my shoulder.

Brain says: Only 355 minutes until we can leave.

"And Cor, if something happens, just text me. You have your cell. You can use it during passing periods, right?"

I nod and hold out my phone to prove that it's on my person and swing my backpack onto my shoulder—it thumps the van.

"Cor, watch the door."

"Just leave," I say, my vocal cords tight like an elastic band, ready to snap.

"Say hi to Mr. Farns," he calls as he pulls away from the curb.

And that is the funniest part because there will be no telling Mr. Farns hi—but Dad and I pretend that I do those things. As his car turns out of sight, I remember that I'm supposed to tell him that Mr. Farns needs his son's car looked at.

I double-knot my shoelaces and wipe the sweat from my upper lip.

Brain says: Today will be worse than Friday.

CHAPTER 11

3 Minutes and 2 Seconds Until I Am Noticeable

*P*aint curls away from The Great Wave like little, dried-up baby waves. Even though the tardy bell has long past rung, someone sits on the grass in front of it—a backpack covered in alien pins and NASA patches beside him.

The kid looks up. His face changes into a smile, a *real* one, one where someone recognizes you in a place they normally don't see you. "Hellloooo!" he says. His lips wide—his teeth horsey . . . it takes me a few seconds. Those teeth . . . that hair. The aloe vera plant. I imagine goggles and a crown.

It's the Aloe Vera Kid from Cat's Cove. His brown hair looks like dandelion fuzz. Like how midnight would look if it exploded in deep space—the blast ending in fuzzy static. In one Big Bad Wolf puff, his hair could fall into a heap around his feet.

"I know you, from yesterday—at the cove, right?" His voice is meant for stadium seating. He follows me. About a dozen key chains hang from the zipper and clack with each step he takes. He's about a foot taller than almost every student.

"Guess what?" he says. His smile's goofy, but sincere. For some reason, he reminds me of Sunshine.

Brain says: Don't stop.

I don't, but I can't help but look back.

He clutches his alien backpack to his chest, like it might rocket him into the atmosphere. "I'm seriously amazing." Then he waves goodbye.

My right hand lifts to shoulder height, and for a second, it almost waves back.

Brain says: I know you haven't lost your mind, because I'm still here.

Room 702, the door to social studies, is almost too heavy to open, but I manage. Mr. Farns doesn't tolerate tardiness with any sort of understanding. I do deep breathing as quietly as I can and pass him perched on a stool near the overhead projector in front of the room. He's typing into his computer. The table I share with three other kids looks full, and I wonder if they were there on Friday when *it* happened.

A kid takes his feet from my empty chair.

"Welcome, Miss Altman," Mr. Farns says.

Why is it so hot in here? I sit and pull up my hood. Protection is necessary. The girl next to me, I can't remember her name, shifts farther away.

Brain says: Going home would be best.

I pull out my social studies journal and begin copying the sentences from the screen.

"Cora," Mr. Farns says. It sounds more like a question than a statement as he fiddles with the projector. "Did you ask your dad about the car?"

All sixty-four eyes turn and stare. They hurt.

Pow. Pow. Pow.

I gulp. I visualize myself smiling. I visualize myself talking. I visualize myself, as Mom likes to say, cool as a cucumber.

Dr. Rosenthal says that if I imagine enough positive actions, someday they'll be real. As real as the timer running constantly through my mind. As real as Brain.

Heat from my face leaks through my body. My arms, chest, neck. I am a human tomato again. Just like—

Friday. *No, not Friday.*

I take a deep breath and nod, even though I didn't talk to Dad about the car.

"We can talk about it later," he says, glancing at the class. "Griffin, switch back to your original seat. Why do we go through this daily? That is not your assigned seat."

"But I like this one." Griffin winks at someone. I can't remember her name, either.

Now the classroom eyes turn to him. *Whew.* Thank goodness for Griffin the troublemaker. I should know, because he went to my elementary school.

Mr. Farns tells everyone we're beginning our World Unit on India. That we're going to watch a clip from YouTube about Indian cotton. He turns off the lights and covers the room in shadow. The tight feeling in my chest loosens a little.

I quickly glance around. Ando Mendez sits in the back of

63

the class, and his eyes are not on YouTube videos about India. His eyes are on me. I don't know what they're trying to say. Minny's much better at reading eyes and all kinds of body language—it's almost her superpower the way she can read people. I feel blind without her.

I pull my hoodie tighter around my face and try to focus on the video. But the feeling of Ando's eyes watching me makes my neck itch.

Ando and Minny were friends. She had lots of friends. Once Mom asked why Minny hadn't rubbed off on me yet.

Brain says: I'm the only one who rubs off on you.

The video continues: "India is the primary producer of the world's cotton . . ."

A cell phone rings.

It rings once. Twice. The noise slices through the silent classroom. Everyone laughs.

Mr. Farns warns, "People, you know the rules." He walks toward my side of the room, but the mystery phone keeps ringing. Why doesn't someone turn it off?

Now Mr. Farns stands in front of my table. The kid at the end squirms in his seat—it's coming from him. Reggie? Arnold? Then a girl elbows me. "Your phone."

"What? No, I don't—"

She holds up my backpack. It's ringing. It *is* my phone. Silently, I blame Dad for making me take it today.

"Cell phones are not to be on during class time," Mr. Farns says gently. We know this. Everyone in class knows this. I was supposed to silence it, but forgot.

He holds his hand out. "You know the rules, Cora. You can get your phone back tomorrow with a note from your parent."

Frantically, I search my black-hole bag—my eyes blur and then fill with water.

The phone blares. Eyeballs stare.

Pow. Pow. Pow.

I dump the contents of my backpack onto the ground. Pens roll down the aisle, a paper floats, books flap, everything sits in one gigantic school supply explosion. I hate everything in my backpack. I hate everyone in this classroom.

I swipe at the tears with one hand and continue to search for the phone with the other.

Someone fake coughs. "Freak."

Mr. Farns says, "That's enough, Griffin. You'll see me after class."

Finally—I see it, stuck between pages of *Tuck Everlasting*.

The ringing stops.

I yank it out and slap it into Mr. Farns's hand, but not before I glance at the screen. A missed call and a new text from Minny. Why would she possibly call me right now?

He looks at me through round eyeglass frames. "Would you like the hall pass?" he asks, I think, sympathetically. "To go to the restroom. Or the nurse?"

I nod. Is every day going to be like Friday? I'm so pitiful.

Brain says: You are.

Kneeling, I shove my books and papers back into my backpack and crunch everything in on top of itself. The pause button on the YouTube video unpauses and begins to play again. Everyone turns back toward the screen. Everyone, that is, except for Ando.

He holds out a pen as I slink past. "You dropped this," he says.

I ignore him and walk out the classroom door.

Brain says: Run.

And so, I do.

CHAPTER 12

11 Minutes and 12 Seconds Until I Change Everything

*K*eeping a wary eye out for Nurse Celebran, who smells of Band-Aids and cranberry juice, I run down the hallway. In the six weeks that I've been here, she's made five phone calls to Mom, when I am—as she likes to put it—"out of sorts."

Brain says: You're definitely out of sorts.

The last thing I need is Mom thundering down to the school, especially when she's upset with Dad, to insist that I am just fine. Or to give me a very gentle lecture on how to deal with my *issues,* while also reminding me to tough it out. There's no way I'm going to the nurse.

Mr. Farns's hall pass, a lime-green wooden spatula, bumps the side of my leg as I run down the hallway. He said he was tired of losing it and thinks color and size will solve the problem.

The front of the school is deserted. My legs feel numb. Panic peeks out through my eyeholes. Why's it so hot? The Great Wave looms. It's just me and the wave. I'd crawl inside it if I could. I'd create a nice little cubby where I could disappear with my treasures and my comforter and Chevy.

A car pulls into a faculty parking space. I inch behind the wave.

It's Mr. Beckett, the vice principal. Sixth grade has only been in session for a little bit, but that's long enough to know that he keeps a large wooden paddle on the wall of his office that says USC. He says it's an antique. But the rumor is he's not afraid to use it—if a parent is at the end of their rope and gives him permission. Minny swears it's true.

My heart vibrates.

Brain says: Run.

Not before Mr. Beckett leaves. Do students who run away from school result in a smack with his paddle?

He stops in front of the wave and answers a call. "Hey, hon," he says.

I hold my breath. What happens to students who hear the vice principal say "hon" into their phone? The curbing around The Great Wave trips me and the weight of my backpack pulls me forward. I land with a squish in the mud.

"Oof!" I say.

Mr. Beckett pokes his head around the wave and his glasses slip down to the tip of his bulbous nose. "Let me call you back."

The mud seeps through the knees of my jeans.

"You startled me." He slides his phone into his shirt pocket. "Cora, right? What're you doing back there?"

The large wooden paddle looms in my mind. Was he here on Friday? I can't remember.

"Here, let me help." He holds out his hand.

Air feels precious, and it is because a giant sits on my chest. Carbon dioxide leaks out of my lungs and they might pop like bubbles in soda.

I place my hand onto the wave for support.

"Are you all right?" he asks. "Here." He grabs my elbow. His fingertips feel like the cafeteria freezer.

"No," I whisper-say.

"Can I call someone for you?" He tugs my elbow between his ice-cube fingers toward the main office. "Come inside. We'll find Nurse Celebran."

Not Nurse Celebran. Her eyes see everything. They say I'm nothing more than a mushroom growing between grass and weeds. The bell rings—the air vibrates with students who have proper lungs and non-talking brains.

I yank my elbow free from Mr. Beckett.

Brain says: Run.

And then—

I do.

I run from a vice principal.

"Hey!" he yells. Mr. Beckett who says "hon" and has freezing Otter Pop fingers and a wooden paddle in his office says, "Stop!"

Like chewed gum being pulled away from paper, my lungs stretch. They stretch and stretch until I fill with air. Taking great gulps, I chug along. Somehow what happened on Friday swims before my eyes.

No matter how I try, I can't stop Brain from thinking it.

FRIDAY

The ground between the 500 and 700 quads at Las Olas Middle School is surprisingly slick. I lie on a smooth disk of space—like some great force has melted the concrete, free from the cracks and lines that cover the rest of the school. Clean from jagged edges or footprints, it's a perfect piece of ground for a hyperventilating girl like me. Normally, I don't lie on the ground at school. But on Friday, I do it for the first time.

Surrounded by students with round, curious mouths and large eggy eyes, I press my back into the division line between the science quad and the English quad and try to breathe, ignoring that I've swallowed the sea. The whole salty cove sloshes around in my belly.

Minny says, "Don't worry, Cora. I'll get help."

Her hand wraps firmly around my wrist. She never leaves my side but makes demands of the people surrounding us. Maybe she hopes I won't notice their eyes. Why's everyone looking at me? Is it because I've burned a hole into the concrete? It's so hot.

Nurse Celebran is here, feeling my forehead and listening to my heart with her ear pressed firmly to my chest.

"Stay back," she says, with her Band-Aid breath, to the students around us.

Am I dying?

Probably. How many seconds will it take? I would tell you, but I don't know. Because right then, the counting inside my head breaks.

I lie there, maybe hours or days. Am I still there, even now, with hundreds of eyes watching my atoms explode? Time is tricky and can get lost. Just like buried treasure.

CHAPTER 13

9 Minutes and 13 Seconds Until the Twin

*B*rain says: Keep running.

So, I do—past the faculty parking lot and onto the sidewalk across the empty street. A lawn mower breaks the silence. Leaves drop from tree branches as I run past, the sea air at my back. This is what happens when Minny is in Florida, sucking oranges out of their skins and laughing with cousins instead of here, protecting me from myself.

Brain says: You should always listen to me.

Even with my stretched-out lungs, it takes me seven minutes and thirteen seconds to get to Aunt Janet's house. Her neighborhood is just around the corner. Heartbeats thunder in my ears—at any moment someone will stop me. School security. The police. Dad. Each hedge or shadowed tree feels dangerous. I'm about to be caught.

But nothing happens.

A dog barks from the corner house on Aunt Janet's street. With each step, I'm a little more free.

Brain says: All good things are wild and free.

Finally, I stand on Aunt Janet's step, in front of her door that's painted a special blue—Blue's blue. Striped awnings sway in the breeze above large front windows, but the best part about Aunt Janet's house is the bougainvillea vines wrapped around her post-lined porch. Her house drips in fuchsia flowers and emerald-green leaves. I've tried counting them before.

Brain says: I don't count foliage.

For a moment, I forget Mom is here until I spy our car parked on the side driveway.

Brain says: She'll make you go back.

A metallic taste rises from my throat. She will. I'll have to be a good soldier, again. And what will Mr. Farns say about my never returning to first period? His spatula hall pass hangs from my wrist.

Brain says: Mr. Farns is a big dumb dummy.

A bougainvillea flower shudders on its stem and drops to the path in front of me, like a splash of raspberry Kool-Aid.

The door swings open. Mom and Aunt Janet stand on the threshold. Sunlight creates a halo around them. Sister twins, but opposite in every way, except for height. Mom light. Aunt Janet dark. Mom serious. Aunt Janet smiles and fun.

I crouch right where I stand on the sidewalk, even though nothing can hide me.

"I'll call you later," Mom says to Aunt Janet, her back to me. Her voice sounds small. She turns. She's still in her green caftan, the one from the night she carried my missing uncle through the door. The one she never wears outside unless it's to quickly check the mail or drive us to school when we're late.

Mom turns. "Cora," she says, surprised.

I stand.

"Cora!" Blue bolts down the walkway and attaches himself to my leg. "Play Hulk-Smash with me!"

Mom's eyes are little slits, like she hasn't slept since . . .

Brain says: Fifty-eight hours—3,480 minutes ago.

She puts on her Mom-face. "What are you doing here?" She puts her arm around me. "Why aren't you at school?" She looks up and down the street. "Did Dad drop you off?"

I shake my head.

"*Cora*, what—?"

I brace for her response, but her mouth snaps closed—her anger bitten in half. She places her hand on her forehead like she's taking her own temperature and sighs as deep as the sea. "You can tell me about it in the car."

Aunt Janet nods reassuringly.

"Okay," I whisper-say.

Where's the speech about how schools aren't a bed of roses and how there's no use crying over spilled milk?

"Call me later," Aunt Janet says to Mom.

Blue tugs at my muddy jeans. "Stay and play."

I shake him free. "Maybe tomorrow, buddy."

I look at Mom, expecting to see her Cora-face: her I'm-exasperated-but-trying-to-hide-it face—but she's not even looking at me. Instead she stares at our car.

"Are you okay?" I ask.

She clicks the car remote, ignoring my question. "Get in."

Brain says: Now you're in for it.

I lug my backpack, with all six of my textbooks, into the car—since sixth graders have to share a locker with an eighth grader "mentor" who's supposed to help you and show you the ropes at Las Olas Middle School. I never use my locker, because I share it with Curtis Pimo and so far, he's mentored me on how to make a locker smell like a beached whale.

Brain says: And look like a natural disaster.

Mom holds up her phone so I can see. "Just checked my phone—the school called *three times*." My stomach knots.

Mom starts the car. She puts on her sunglasses and listens to the messages. "Cora, they sound panicked. Why didn't you go to Nurse Celebran? We worked it out on Friday. Dr. Rosenthal said if you felt an attack coming on, that was the plan. Right? *We all* decided that's what you'd do."

It's so easy. It all should be so easy.

Brain says: Nurse Celebran can go eat some more Band-Aids.

Mom whips her sunglasses off and stares at me. Her brown eyes are flecked with gold, but the dark circles underneath make me worried. She pulls onto the road.

The silence inside the car is so loud.

1 2 3 4 5

I count fuzz balls on the floor mat.

She pulls down the street then turns left, *toward* my school.

I will vomit.

Mom pushes speed dial on the car's hands-free device and

puts in her earbuds. "Yes, I'd like to speak to Principal Shurtzer. Yes, this is Mrs. Altman, Cora's mother."

Oh no, not Dr. Principal Marilyn Shurtzer.

There's a pause. Then, "Hi. Hello. Yes, I have her."

Mom listens.

"No, I don't think so. We'll have her evaluated again. Yes. Yes. We'd prefer to handle it with our own doctor. I'm so sorry for the scare. Thank you for understanding."

Mom listens some more.

Brain says: 99.9 percent of the kids at that school want to run away, you were just brave enough to do it.

"Yes, I'll let you know what our plan is for tomorrow. We do—we realize how serious this is. I'll be in touch. Goodbye."

She pushes a button on the car. "They were this close to calling the police."

Brain says: So, call the police! That school is a prison.

I imagine Vice Principal Beckett's paddle. Is Mom at the end of her rope? Is she exasperated enough to give him permission to give me a few smacks?

Brain says: I'd say so. Yes.

"Cora, what were you thinking?"

I bite my lip.

"Something must have happened. Was someone mean to you?"

I shake my head.

"Was it another panic attack?"

I don't respond.

She sighs loudly. "You can be so frustrating. I can't help if you won't talk to me." As our car turns away from the school, she pushes on the gas—hard.

I hold my breath. "Are you taking me home?" I ask in a small voice, hoping the question doesn't change her mind.

"Sunshine has Early Out today. I have to pick her up now."

"Sunshine? Why does she have Early Out?"

Mom ignores me.

We pull into the parking lot of Sunshine's elementary school.

"Wait here." She walks up the sidewalk and ducks through the school's front door.

Sunshine bursts out of the school with a smile almost as large as her backpack. Mom follows, her caftan floating behind her as she tries not to collide with Sunshine's zigzagging.

Breathless, Sunshine flings open the car door. "We're going to IHOP!"

"Nooo." I put my hands over my face. Not Social Skills.

Brain says: Ordering pancakes can't help you survive this world.

Sunshine crawls over me to get into the back seat and squishes my hand with her heel.

"Sunshine! Go through your own door," I snap.

"I'm getting chocolate chip pancakes." Her eyes sparkle as she pulls a stuffed animal from her backpack and swings it through the air.

"You can't take toys to school," I say, and then immediately regret it because I sound like Mom.

"Yes, I can because today was All About Me Day and I'm

allowed to bring Mr. Freckles on my special day." She pulls a crumpled-up poster from her backpack and leans over me to flatten it out on my lap. "See, I drew a picture of him right here." She jabs at her picture as her chubby finger pokes my thigh. "I want chocolate chip pancakes, Mommy!"

Mom slides into the driver's seat. "You got it." Her sunglasses glint in the sun.

"Why Social Skills?" I whine.

"Apparently, you need it."

My heart bumps.

I try again. "Aren't we going home so you can change?"

She looks down at her outfit and shrugs.

Brain says: Aliens, I tell you.

"I like Mommy's dress." Sunshine's smile is so very sunny. "It feels like vacation."

I'm acutely aware of how Sunshine changes all the protons and electrons around her into happiness.

"What's on your lap?" she asks, eyeing Mr. Farns's spatula bracelet.

"Nothing." I shove it into my backpack.

"I want to wear it."

"No."

"Do you get to do cooking at school?"

"No."

Mom pulls out of the parking space. "Who wants breakfast with whipped cream?"

"Me! Me! Me!" Sunshine bounces and the car shakes back and forth.

"You never take us to IHOP during school." I feel a little seasick.

"After recent events, today *requires* a visit to IHOP. You're both coming. Plus, I haven't seen you since Saturday."

In Mom's opinion, IHOP is the perfect place to do all the things I hate, like looking people in the eye, speaking up, telling people what I want, or small talk with strangers. Social Skills bites.

"Why didn't you come home last night?" I ask.

Mom stares out the windshield, ignoring me.

Sunshine nods solemnly. "Yes, Mommy. I missed you so much. Where were you?"

"At Aunt Janet's." Mom slaps on a fake smile as she pulls into the parking lot.

Sunshine asks, "Can I get bacon?"

Mom's plastic smile says, "Of course."

Brain says: A little bacon might perk us all up.

No, Brain. You can't be on Mom's side.

A lady walks across the parking lot pushing a cart full of bottles.

Mom opens her door. The smell of pancakes wafts through the car, and my stomach gurgles.

"Any glass?" The lady stops, her voice grainy. A bandanna covers her long gray braids; she looks toasted by ultraviolet rays. Her overalls are too small, and she wears tap shoes, *real* tap shoes on her feet, that make short, clacking sounds every time she moves.

Sunshine is entranced.

Where am I supposed to look? I hate being around people I don't know, especially weird ones.

"I take bottles too," says the woman.

Sunshine gets out of the car. "Baby bottles?"

"Plastic bottles," the woman says. "And cans. Got any cans?"

"I'm sorry, no." Mom motions for me to get out of the car, but I shake my head.

"Wait, wait. I do!" Sunshine opens the back door and pulls out the plastic water bottle from her lunch box. She loosens the cap and turns it over—water splashes her feet as she empties it onto the pavement. "Here." She hands it to the lady. "And some money, too, right, Mommy?"

"Let me see." Mom fumbles around in her purse.

"The bottle's fine." But the lady isn't looking at Mom. She looks at me. Her eyes bore into mine like laser beams.

Brain says: Take a picture, it lasts longer.

"God bless," she says, and tap-dances her cart away.

Under my burning skin, I wonder what the tap-dancing lady saw. Does she know I'm a human tomato? Can she tell that no one at school likes me?

The IHOP sign glints high above us.

"Come on, Cora. Sunshine, onward. Those pancakes aren't going to eat themselves!" Mom's fake cheeriness is not lost on me. Is this all because Dad's missing brother is back? Or a punishment because I ran away from school? Why's Mom acting weird?

"This is the best day ever!" exclaims Sunshine.

CHAPTER 14

8 Minutes Until Mom Comes Clean

*E*ven from the waiting area, I feel the stares of every person in the restaurant. I feel their heartbeats thumping in their chests. I feel their strangerness.

Brain says: Four thousand square feet covered in sticky judgment.

As the door closes behind me, I quickly scan the restaurant—seven people, not including us. My heart thunders and my hands begin to shake. Please, no one look at me. I turn to Mom. "Not today." I grab the flowy ends of her caftan and ball the fabric up in my fists, slick with sweat.

Mom puts her arm around my shoulder, but she keeps her eyes forward. She says quietly into my ear, "It's not busy. You'll be fine. Someday you'll thank me for this. You can't avoid everything in the world, Cora." She smiles at the hostess like everything's fine. I hate Social Skills.

"Welcome to IHOP," says the hostess lady. She has

grandma hair and a name tag that says *Dora*. She smiles at Mom, then at me, and then at Sunshine.

I clasp my hands together to keep them from shaking.

"How many in your party?"

My mind goes blank.

Mom waits.

Sunshine says, "We want pancakes!"

Dora nods and shuffles menus into her arms. "How many?"

I gulp. I'm a tomato, a human tomato. What am I supposed to say again?

Mom tips her head toward me, so patient, like we have all the time in the world.

The door opens behind us and in walk a man and a little girl.

Mom whispers, "Come on, Cora. You can do it."

I tremble.

Sunshine says, "Can I have some crayons?"

Dora hands her crayons. "My name's Dora if you need anything."

"Hey, Cora, her name rhymes with yours. Cora and Dora." She giggles.

Dora smiles. "Three then?"

"One, two, three!" says Sunshine, pointing at each of us. "And I want chocolate chip pancakes!"

We follow Dora to our table. "Three it is for chocolate chip pancakes."

Mom links her pinkie with mine. "It's okay. Next time."

I pull away.

Sunshine slides into the booth. "I'm five and in kindergarten and today was my special day at school."

"Well, isn't that the bee's knees." Dora sets our menus on the table.

Sunshine laughs. "Bees don't have knees."

"Why not?" she asks. "People do. Your waiter will be right over." She smiles as she walks away. Another member of the Sunshine fan club.

Smudges of sticky jam cover my side of the table.

Brain says: Animals.

I set my hands in my lap.

Mom and Sunshine sit on one side and me on the other. I do deep breathing and fan myself with my menu.

Mom plops her menu onto the tabletop. "Cora, you can't let Sunshine do all the talking."

Sunshine peers at me over her menu plastered with pictures of eggs and bacon and whipped cream. "Why not?" she asks. "I like talking."

My stomach twists. There's no way I can eat anything here.

When the waiter comes, I let Sunshine order for both of us. Mom doesn't say anything. When she thinks I don't notice, she looks at me with sad eyes. When our food comes, I push the bloated, syrup-soaked, chocolate chip pancakes around on my plate with my fork.

"You should've just ordered the strawberry French toast, like you like," Mom says.

"These are fine," I mumble.

"Can I have your leftovers?" asks Sunshine, her mouth covered in syrup and cream.

I push my plate over to her.

"You need to eat something," Mom says.

"I can't eat here."

Mom scoops some of her eggs onto a smaller plate and pushes it toward me. "Here."

Brain says: You hate eggs.

Finally, I say, "Mom, what's going on? Why didn't you come home this weekend?"

"Dad and I were having a disagreement."

"Why? You knew Dad had another brother, right?"

"Yes, of course. He lived with us when you were a baby."

Sunshine interrupts. "Uncle Joaquin used to live with us?"

Mom shakes her head. "Eat your pancakes, sweetie." She pokes at Sunshine's messy face with a napkin.

Sunshine jerks away.

"He did?" I stop fiddling with my fork.

"For six months."

Brain says: Call me stunned.

Naturally, Mom and Dad know things I don't, but I still feel a little betrayed that until today, no one has mentioned that he lived with us. I thought Dad said he hadn't seen him since he was twelve.

A memory from when I was in first grade now makes sense. Christmas dinner was eaten, the dessert was gone, and I had opened all my gifts. Everyone had. The living room was strewn with empty boxes and wrapping paper, but I spied one gift tucked behind the tree. It looked so lonely, squished against the wall.

Brain interrupts: There's nothing worse than unopened presents.

I'd yanked the present free and waved it in front of my grandma's face. "Vo, is this mine? Did you forget to give this to me?"

But she'd shaken her head and set the box high on top of the fridge. "No, Cora. That's for my boy." I thought she meant Dad or Uncle Joaquin, but now I see she meant my missing uncle. That present stayed unopened every year.

Mom's cell dings. She doesn't check it. Instead she crosses her utensils over her plate, a signal that she's done.

The waiter comes toward us. My heartbeat quickens. I stare at the strawberry jam as he sets the bill on the table.

"Thank you." Mom takes the check.

I wait until he leaves. "Why didn't anyone ever talk about Dad's missing brother?"

"He wasn't, exactly, good to us."

My uncle isn't good?

She takes a sip of ice water. "I'm sure your dad will have more to say on the subject and we'll get to all that, but first, I owe you an apology."

An apology? I put my fork down.

"I'm sorry I disappeared to Aunt Janet's."

I nod, because what can you say when your mom apologizes?

"It was such a shock when he called. And then he was, well, *you know*, when Dad picked him up." She continues, eyeing Sunshine. "Your dad thinks it's best to let bygones be bygones, but I don't know if I can." She sighs, and the darkness under her eyes seems darker. "But as for you running away from school today, Dad and I are going to have to discuss it. It's Block Day. You only have two more classes until school's out."

PE and math.

Brain says: This is not the time for sweating and equations.

She looks at her watch. "I guess you don't have to go back to school, but tomorrow we have a meeting with the principal."

That night, when Dad gets home, he comes into my room as Sunshine and I are sprawled across my bed reading. Chevy's got his head on my stomach.

He stands in the doorway. "Cor-Bell, really?" His eyebrows raise into a question, his hands on his hips.

My heart bumps.

"Daddy!" yells Sunshine, jumping off my bed into his arms.

"Hi, baby girl." He gives her a hug. "Why don't you go see what Mom's up to in the living room? Then we'll play Tickle Monster when I'm done talking with Cora."

Sunshine giggles wildly. "I'm going to win!" She runs out the door. She can't resist the game where Dad turns off all the lights in the house and hides. Growling like a bear, he chases and tickles us until we almost pee our pants. In the history of the game Tickle Monster, I've peed my pants three times.

Brain says: You're too old for baby games.

Dad sits and puts his arm around me. "My main concern is you. Are you okay?"

I nod. A lump forms in my throat. It'd be better if he were mad just like Mom.

"What made you leave school without permission? You said you'd call me if you were stressed out."

Brain says: He won't understand.

Dad's eyes are soft. "Not ready to talk about it?"

Mom rounds the corner, Sunshine trailing behind her. "You're going to have to talk about it eventually, Cora."

"But we don't have to push her if she isn't feeling up to it."

Mom glares at him and marches down the hall to her room.

Dad's smile is grim. "It's going to be fine. Don't worry." He follows Mom and their door snaps shut.

"Maybe they're talking about Christmas presents." Sunshine's eyes brighten.

"Maybe." I pull her up onto my bed and tuck my arm around her. Even though I read Sunshine's picture book out loud, I still listen for my name in the argument that bleeds from underneath their door.

Chevy barks into the air. He feels it too. We try to drown out the resentment spreading from their side of the house.

CHAPTER 15

Tuesday: 15 Minutes and 10 Seconds Until I Get a Forced Friend Who Makes Me Sick

*T*he next morning, the principal's office is so cold that Mom gives me her cardigan, which I lay across my bare legs.

Brain says: Goose bumps are leftover reflexes from when humans had long body hair.

Dr. Shurtzer's office is surprisingly small, but a wide window looks out onto The Great Wave surrounded by a sea of emerald grass. There isn't a paddle on her wall, like the vice principal's, just framed papers with fancy writing and her name, Marilyn G. Shurtzer.

Mom's smile is wide, making her teeth gleam. It's the one she reserves for when she's apologizing for me. Dr. Shurtzer's and Mom's smiles match.

This morning, Dad explained that his brother really needs him today at detox, but I need him too—with his bright smile and handsome Dad-face. He wins over people at the grocery store, and at the bank, and at school, by making everything easy. Aunt Janet calls it charm. But I think it's just because he listens to people and acts like he cares. It's one of his best dad-qualities.

Brain says: Are you sure you're related?

Nine minutes and thirteen seconds have passed since we came into Dr. Shurtzer's office.

Mom clears her throat.

Today, I have Mom. And she hasn't stopped talking since we sat down. She's talked about my anxiety, my social worries, Brain, my therapist, and what my pediatrician thinks. I sit here, in this wooden chair, and appear to be conscious.

In the car, Mom said it would be like presenting an olive branch if I apologized for leaving school without permission. Ancient Greeks used the olive branch to symbolize peace. Are Dr. Principal Marilyn Shurtzer and I in a fight?

Brain says: We don't talk to principals and we don't apologize.

Once, when I accidentally used the wrong ribbon in the gift wrap station at Aunt Janet's store, I had to apologize. "This gift is for a *boy*," the customer had said in a loud voice—and I had to rewrap, and it took an extra six minutes, and the customer kept looking at her gold watch and sighing loudly.

I said sorry to that lady.

And to Aunt Janet.

But Aunt Janet said it was fine and that boy babies should get to have any old color of wrapping paper for their gifts and that the rule of pink for girls and blue for boys was archaic.

Brain says: I prefer a deep aqua.

"Cora," says Mom. "You have to promise to check in with Nurse Celebran daily."

I hesitate.

"And she wants you to give your word that you won't leave campus again without permission."

I nod.

Dr. Shurtzer says, "I really must get your promise on this, Cora. We have very strict safety protocols at our school. At Las Olas Middle School, we are responsible for your well-being while you're on this campus. I'm afraid I won't let behavior like this slide again. There will be consequences, like in-school suspension." Her eyes look huge through her thick red-framed glasses, which are held around her neck by a gold chain. She pulls off her glasses—they fall to her chest with a thunk.

My heart bumps. She thinks I'm a delinquent.

Brain says: You are.

"Can I have your word?" Dr. Shurtzer asks again. She plays with the chain attached to her glasses. Her smile hurts.

"Cora." Mom's eyes narrow. She gently squeezes my knee.

"You won't leave campus without going through the proper protocols?" Dr. Principal, Marilyn G. Shurtzer, asks. She nods at me like I belong in kindergarten with Sunshine. "I'll really need verbal confirmation that you understand, Cora."

I croak out, "Yes." My face thrums with heat. I hate it when Dr. Principal Marilyn Shurtzer looks at me.

"And one last thing," she says. "We've paired you with

another student for the month, just to help you get better settled . . . since Minny moved."

Everything inside my head halts. All the seconds stop.

Mom adds, "When I spoke to Dr. Rosenthal about it over the phone last night, she agreed it was a good idea."

I have to have a *forced friend*? Brain is shocked into silence.

Now I've got to hang out with some kid who's been ordered to be nice to me, but behind my back, she'll roll her eyes and call me freak?

"No," I sputter.

"Nevertheless, it's all arranged." The principal presses a button on her intercom. "Diane, can you send Patrick in, please?"

Patrick—a boy?! Oh, where's Minny when I need her?

Mom adjusts her necklace. "How nice. I knew a Patrick when I was your age."

Brain says: Well that makes everything just peachy.

The door bangs open.

I jump.

It's the kid with the goggles and the alien pins. The *I'm amazing* weirdo. The Aloe Vera Kid.

Diane, the receptionist, peeks out from behind him. "I'm sorry, he was so eager to get inside."

"I knew it was you!" he says, pumping his fist into the air. "See! We're supposed to be friends."

CHAPTER 16

2 Minutes and 12 Seconds Until I Find Out That Patrick Is Abnormally Happy

"*I*t'll be fine." Mom kisses the top of my head. "And I'm making your favorite, orange chicken, for dinner tonight."

Brain says: I'll believe it when I see it.

"I love orange chicken!" Patrick holds his hand up to give me a high five. I pretend I don't see it.

Mom nods politely, and even I can tell she thinks he's a little much. She hands me my phone she picked up from Mr. Farns before our meeting with the principal.

Patrick says, "Don't worry about a thing. Cora's going to have a *great* day! I'll make sure of it!" He follows us out the door, his backpack jangling with alien hardware.

Mom says, "Don't forget to put your phone on silent."

Brain says: How do we put this kid on silent?

Mom gives me a thumbs-up. "You catch more flies with honey than with vinegar."

Brain says: Who wants to catch flies?

"Have a good day, sweetheart," Mom says. My face burns as she walks out the door.

Patrick waves a paper in my face. "See, they already gave me your schedule. I can walk you to every class." He holds his hand up to give me another high five, which I ignore—again.

"You're not into high fives? Cool."

I don't respond.

He peers at my schedule. "Darn, we don't have any classes together." He honestly sounds bummed.

As we walk through the crowded hall toward my locker, I wish I could disappear into the concrete.

"What were you doing at Cat's Cove on Sunday?" he asks.

Brain says: That's *our* cove.

Patrick continues, "I was there with my friends, doing some important research for an exciting project I have on the horizon."

Patrick doesn't seem to mind that I don't answer. He's too busy calling exuberant helllooos to every person we pass.

Some kids say hi, while others ignore him and roll their eyes.

My face burns. In nineteen seconds, we reach my choir classroom and I breathe a sigh of relief.

Patrick calls, "Have no fear, Cora! I'll be right here after class."

Brain says: I've never wanted a natural disaster more in my life.

In choir, I sit in the very back. My academic adviser thought this class might be good for "helping Cora come out of her shell." Even Dr. Rosenthal agreed. Mom was thrilled. Dad thought I might do better in orchestra. Every kid at my school must take some form of music in their sixth-grade year. At least in choir I can blend into the background without being noticed.

Brain loves choir.

Brain says: Singing is a declaration of the joy within.

If I could sing about my metal detector, or The Cat's treasure, then I'd sing all day long, but no one writes songs about that. Brain doesn't care what kind of song we're singing—he loves all of them.

Mr. Tribalty stands in front of the room and claps his hands. "Come in, my little waves. Come rolling in to sing with vigor." He sits at the piano and plays the *Jaws* theme song to get everyone's attention. He does this every time we have class.

Ba—dum. Ba—dum. Ba-dum badumbadum.

He thinks it's hilarious.

Brain says: It is.

It takes twenty-seven seconds for the class to calm down.

Mr. Tribalty's fingers move across the piano without him even looking down. How would it feel to be that good at something?

The room vibrates with the energy of fifty-four sixth graders. I slide into my folding chair and stare at my shoes so I don't have to talk to the kid on my right, Delaney, who was in my class in the fourth grade. I don't know the other kid on my left.

"Revolting children, today we shall begin with 'Revolting Children,'" says Mr. Tribalty.

Everyone laughs.

We're singing "Revolting Children" from the musical *Matilda*. It's about children who are downtrodden and bullied by their school's headmistress, Miss Trunchbull. It's a fun song—if I liked choir and if I liked to sing.

I bet Patrick loves choir.

Delaney says, "Scoot your chair over. You're practically on top of me." The bracelets around her wrist jingle. She wears three gold ones and a leather wrap.

I move my chair over two inches because it's as far as I can go without bumping into the boy on the other side of me.

"You're Minny's friend, aren't you?" she asks. Delaney never remembers my name. Her bangs are stuck in her eyelashes. I hate her looking at me. Immediately my pulse increases. I take a big gulp of air. Minny always smiles when she talks to people.

Delaney says. "Is she here today or did she move already?"

I look at the floor and shake my head as heat rises to my face, which only means I'm turning into a human fireball. I pretend Minny's sitting right next to me—*Come on, Cora, it's not that bad*, she'd say.

Brain says: Don't smile now, you'll look crazy.

"What's your name again?" Delaney probably thinks she's being nice to me, but if she would just stop talking and pay attention to the teacher, then that would make me feel so much better.

I widen my eyes and try to speak, but it sounds more like a bark. "Cora."

"What?" she asks over Mr. Tribalty's pounding piano.

Bum de-bum. Bum.

"CORA!" I say, just as the music stops.

Six kids turn and stare.

Mr. Tribalty looks up from the piano. "Everything okay, girls?"

Delaney nods. "Okeydokey, Mr. T." She gives him a thumbs-up and me the side-eye with a look—weirdo.

My face burns.

"Cora, you okay?" asks Mr. Tribalty.

I nod and wipe my palms on my pants. The top of my head pulses with heat.

"Okay, then," he says.

The class turns back around.

"Let's start at stanza four." He taps his baton on the music stand.

Delaney turns to the girl sitting next to her and soon they giggle. The music continues, but I don't sing. In case Mr. Tribalty looks in my direction, I mouth the words.

Music is the worst. I hate this class.

The class sings: "Revolting children, alive in bad times, we sing horrible ballads."

Brain says: Revolting children can't change who they are.

CHAPTER 17

16 Minutes Until Dad Has Show-and-Tell

After school Patrick says, "I know we're going to be *best* friends." We stand in front of The Great Wave; the grass area is flooded with students. "I can tell these things. My grandma says I have a sixth sense. A gift." He nods fervently.

I don't respond.

My last class ended four and a half minutes ago. I feel the whole school's eyes on us. I can imagine what they're thinking. Freak One and Freak Two. Doesn't Patrick have friends of his own?

I pull up my hoodie.

"Usually I ride my bike home with DJ and Marco because we live near each other." He nods his head toward the bike racks. "But I don't see—wait, there they are." He stands on his tiptoes and waves. "Hey, guys," he yells in his Patrick-sized voice.

Two boys hunch down and unlock their bikes quickly.

Patrick yells, "I can't ride home today because—"

The boys roll their bikes around the corner, pretending they don't hear him.

Patrick shrugs. "Sometimes they do that." He smiles. "I guess they gotta go."

Brain says: Take us with you.

So, we stand and wait. Patrick waits with me while I turn into a tomato.

"Can you come over to my house?" he asks.

I feel myself burning brighter. "My dad," I say, and wave at a car slowing to a stop in front of the pickup line. It's not my dad. I take a few steps toward the car.

"Okay, see you tomorrow, buddy." Patrick holds his hand up to give me a high five. I don't slap it. Finally, he turns away, pushing against the tide of kids like grunion—fish swimming out of the sea to spawn on dry ground. I can still hear his booming HELLOS as he disappears into the crowd.

Grateful that Mom brought my bike in the back of her car this morning, I grab it from the bike racks and head toward Custom Ride, Dad's shop.

The back door is wide open. Music bounces off the walls, which means Javier is here today. He doesn't notice me as I slink past the car up on blocks and head for Dad's office. He's older than Dad and the backbone of the business (that's what Dad says). Javier has a habit of trying to pat my head and say that I'm getting taller than Mimi, his wife—who's the nicest lady ever, unless you hate seafood. Then she won't stop hounding you until she converts you with her shrimp ceviche.

I knock and push the door open at the same time. Dad's

on the phone, of course, just like always. I don't think he's stopped talking on it since his missing brother came back.

He holds up his hand. "One sec, Cor. Go help Javier. I'll be out soon."

I know for a fact it won't be one second; it's already been five. Even with his hand over the speaker, I can hear Mom yelling. She's still mad about the resurrection of Uncle #2.

"Cor-Bell, I'll be out in a second."

I leave the door slightly ajar because—well, because maybe I want to hear what they're talking about.

Minny loved coming to Custom Ride. She always did this funny, jumpy dance to Javier's music.

I check my phone. What was the text she sent while I was in Mr. Farns's class yesterday?

Minny texted: Gd luck at school today!

Ugh. That definitely wasn't a good-luck text.

I text: You too. How was your first day?

I hesitate.

I text: But don't text me at school. I just got my phone out of phone jail.

Dad's showroom glows in the late afternoon sun as cars and pedestrians pass the gigantic windows. Two vintage roadsters gleam, framed in light, so important, bigger than special. Everything Dad touches turns into treasure.

Brain says: Except you.

Javier sees me. "Cora, the school day is over? Good! You're where you should be—fueling our *great company*." He pounds his chest with gusto. He has an extreme reverence for cars.

I smile and nod.

Javier always talks like that. Together, he and Dad rule the world—at least the world of Custom Ride. He pulls me over to a workbench for his favorite game: *What Can Cora Fix?* He dumps out a small box of parts and walks away. "Five minutes," he calls over his shoulder.

"Less," I say, how I'm supposed to respond. But I don't feel like playing our game today. I stare at the parts and half-heartedly pick up a coil of wire and imagine if Patrick were here. He'd never stop bouncing and talking—annoying Javier.

Finally, Dad comes out of his office. "I want to show you something. I think you'll get a kick out of it."

I turn toward the showroom, expecting him to pick out one of his newest creations.

"Not there." He pulls me toward the office. His desk, like always, is covered in paperwork. Javier's desk is pristine. Dad moves a stack on top of another stack, looking for something. And before I can ask him if Mom's still mad, he asks, "How was school today?"

Why do we have to ruin a perfectly good afternoon by talking about school?

"Fine."

Dad gives me a look. "Mom said you made a new, um, *friend*." I can tell by his eyes he's amused.

"This morning I thought Mom wasn't talking to you."

He bows deeply, with a flourish. "The silent treatment is over."

Brain says: Now it's the yelling treatment.

I sit on the corduroy couch. "The principal's punishing me for leaving school without permission yesterday."

Dad says, "A friend is a punishment? I seem to recall that working out for you before."

"When?" I ask.

"You remember when your second-grade teacher asked Minny to be your special friend?"

I start. "That's not true. We became friends because we both liked geckos."

"Oh, that's right," says Dad. "My mistake." He disappears behind an open cabinet.

I shake off what he said. Minny wasn't my forced friend. But then I remember all the animals she brought home. One time she had a cat, four kittens, a baby bird that fell out of its nest, a frog she found in a dry streambed, and a dog with a limp. Minny couldn't walk away from an animal or a friend in need.

Dad interrupts my thoughts. "You should bring your new friend to the shop."

"Dad, he's not my friend."

He raises his eyebrows.

"How's Uncle Number Two?" I ask.

"You mean Richard? You can call him Uncle Richie."

Uncle Richie. He looked like a mix between Dad and Uncle Joaquin.

"Uncle Joaquin wants to come out to see Richie. But I told him to hold off until he gets out of detox because there's nothing he can do right now."

Now it's my turn to raise my eyebrows.

He takes a deep breath. "Cor—" He swallows what he's going to say. "Tomorrow's a new day. Baby steps, right? Two steps forward, one step back."

I nod. Lately, every step feels like a step back.

Dad pulls out a shoebox wrapped in newspaper and duct tape from the cabinet. The right side is crushed. "You'll think this is interesting. I found it in the garage."

"What is it?"

"You do understand the concept of a surprise, right?" Dad's eyes twinkle. It's not hard to imagine him at Sunshine's age.

Words zigzag across the top in black marker:

Keep Out.

Do You Want Your Eyes Gouged Out?

Yes, I'm Talking to You.

"You want me to open a box that's threatening me?"

He nods.

I shake it.

"Open it or I'll give it to Sunshine."

I untape the lid. Inside it's musty, like the old game closet at Grandma Bell's house, before she had to move to a nursing home. I sift through a random collection of things. Papers, a string of metal tags, two photos, an ID, a small notebook, and a chunk of rusty metal.

Dad spills everything onto his desk.

"It's the time capsule I made in Mr. Farns's sixth-grade class." He sounds triumphant.

I pick up an old Las Olas student ID. "Is this *you*?" A kid with shoulder-length, wavy hair stares back at me.

Brain says: That's definitely a girl.

"Yep." Dad laughs. "Should I grow it out again?"

"Mom would kill you."

Dad shrugs.

It could be a photo of Sunshine. It's weird how much she and Dad look alike, with matching tall foreheads and crinkles at the corners of their eyes, like they're about to burst out laughing.

Dad grabs the card and clucks at the picture. "Vo was always itching to cut it."

"Why didn't she?" Mom would never let something as obvious as weirdo hair ruin my chance to blend in.

"She had bigger things to worry about."

"Like Uncle Richie running away?"

"It was hard on all of us," Dad agrees.

How would I feel if Sunshine went missing?

"Why is Mom mad he's back?" I ask.

He hesitates. "She blames him for . . . for not being who he should've been."

"And you don't?"

"I think it's better to judge someone on what they're doing right now. Not their past."

"Mom said he lived with us. You didn't tell me that."

He folds his arms across his chest. "That was a long time ago, when we were first married." He presses his lips together. "It's complicated. What else did she say?"

"That's all." I continue shuffling through his time capsule. I don't like being in the middle of Mom and Dad when they're not getting along.

He picks up an old school newspaper. "Just know, Cora, sometimes people make mistakes and it's our job to figure out how to forgive them. Everyone deserves forgiveness."

Brain says: What did Uncle Richie do?

I pick up a photo of Dad. He's surrounded by a group of boys and girls squinting into the afternoon sun. They stand arm in arm on the jetty—the moment caught mid-spray, right as a wave crashes into the rocks behind, drenching them all. They laugh like it's the funniest thing ever.

Brain says: Like best friends.

Like best friends forever. My hearts thumps.

Dad holds out the chunk of metal. "Check this out. It's from the night of the plane crash."

The billionaire? The treasure? "You never told me about this."

"Yeah, I did."

I shake my head. "I would've remembered."

"I guess I forgot about it. Uncle Richie reminded me of the time capsule."

He hands me the hunk of metal, obviously part of something much larger. It's heavy and so rusted it leaves reddish flakes on my hands and jeans.

"What is it?"

"Wreckage." Dad looks sly.

"What?!" Am I actually holding a piece of The Cat's plane?

Dad sits on the overstuffed couch next to me.

People in La Quinta Beach heard about the crash in the news, but that's when the rest of the story gets muddy.

"The police found the wreckage and some of her belongings, but a body was never recovered," Dad begins.

"But do you *really* think she traveled with gold coins?"

Dad nods. "Maybe. People say she was eccentric. It's believable."

Everyone who lives in La Quinta Beach has an opinion.

But I've done my research.

Most theories are far-fetched, like Catherine Van Larr lives with one hundred cats in Ecuador, or she lives hidden in plain sight, working at Stuffed Pizza downtown with her hair dyed. One even claims she has amnesia and has taken on a new identity.

I've read all the news and the blogs, but most theories seem unlikely. The only one that's good is *Nine Lives*. It's the smartest. The author says he has evidence that The Cat always traveled with a large amount of gold coins. Why? Because she didn't trust anyone.

Dad pushes his door all the way closed. "Twenty-five years ago, I was at La Quinta Beach hunting grunion with my best friend, Guzman."

I hold the metal in my lap. Ruva would go crazy to find a hunk like this.

"Uncle Richie had been gone for a few months. My family had done everything we could to find him, but it was like he disappeared into thin air. Vo took it the worst. Even though she tried to carry on for my brother and me, I heard her cry every day."

Poor Vo. Heartbroken.

"That night, Guzman and I had gathered more grunion than we could carry. We took the beach trail home, trading off lugging the bucket. When out of nowhere, someone ran by, knocking the bucket out of my grasp and spilling the fish everywhere."

Dad runs his hands through his hair.

"I yelled, 'Watch it!'—and then a voice said, 'Go home, Paulo.' It sounded like Richie. I idolized him. I couldn't believe it. Right at that moment something zoomed across the sky, so loud that both Guzman and I dropped to our knees. Then there was a loud explosion. Fire trucks and ambulances soon followed. I tried to find Richie, but he was gone. I hoped that he'd finally come home, but he never did."

My eyes must be huge because Dad puts his arm around me.

"That was the last night I saw my brother, until you were a baby. Later we heard on the news that it was Catherine Van Larr's plane. The police couldn't figure it out. No Catherine. No black box. No nothing. It was like the plane was flown by remote."

Or a ghost.

Brain says: I don't believe in ghosts.

After the crash, people say they've seen a cat wandering

the beach at night—Catherine Van Larr—searching for her lost treasure.

Dad picks up the metal chunk. "The next day Guzman and I found this at the jetty." His eyes sparkle and I can see the boy he was in the ID card at Las Olas Middle School. Probably he was the king of everything. Probably he was just like Ando.

Shivers run down the back of my legs. The thing I lost at Cat's Cove on Sunday, could it be The Unattainable Find? Was it a gold coin? With all the storms we've had, the treasure could've been stirred to the surface.

"Dad," I say. "I found something on Sunday. I know it has something to do with The Cat—I just feel it." I wrap my fingers around his wrist.

He puts the metal back into his time capsule. "The treasure's out there, Cora. We're going to find it."

Dad and I can do this—we can do it together.

His cell rings. He checks the number and answers it instantly. "This is Paulo."

I squeeze his wrist. "Dad," I whisper-say.

"Yes, he's checking in tomorrow." His voice is pinched. There's *blah blah blah* talking from the other end.

"I'm the cosigner," he says. "But I haven't given my permission for that. No. Let me speak to him." Dad mutes the phone. "Cor, I can't go right now. You go home and I'll hear about it tonight."

He pats my hand and goes back to his call. Blast that Uncle Richie.

"Sounds great, Dad." But my feet know where they're going.

Brain says: You are turning into a good liar.

I grab Ruva Mom left for me at Custom Ride.

Minny texts: Sry about your phone my new neighbor reminds me of u

CHAPTER 18

27 Minutes and 3 Seconds Until I Have a Guest

I have to get back to Cat's Cove. Hot pink drips into the water as the sun sinks halfway into the ocean. Trash litters the beach, but it's only lightly sprinkled with people. By now, most have headed home. It's the perfect time for treasure hunting.

My heart thumps. Nothing seems more important than the lost thing—not Mom, or Dad, or Blue, or Aunt Janet, or mysterious Uncle Richie. I need that Unattainable Find.

Mom and Dad will be so proud. "We always knew there was something special about our Cora," they'd say. I'd be The Girl Who Found The Cat's Treasure. Dr. Principal Marilyn Shurtzer will give me a certificate with a golden seal and let me leave campus anytime I want. At IHOP, they'll already know my favorite breakfast and I'll never have to order out loud again.

I look out at the bay. Underneath the water lies an artificial reef created from hundreds of sunken vessels. Those ships didn't sink here, like a Californian Bermuda Triangle. They used to litter oceans all over the world, but then the wreckage was brought here. Once a year La Quinta city adds to the reef. A barge floats into the harbor with demolished pieces to add to the collection of shattered fiberglass, rusted engines, and waterlogged wood. Catherine Van Larr's wrecked plane is somewhere out there too.

Brain says: Slathered with gold.

My bike bumps down the trail toward Cat's Cove. Where was I treasure hunting on Sunday? How much does sand shift?

Brain says: It depends on storms and rain level.

Since Minny left, I've hardly felt like myself. But now, as I breathe in the salty air, I feel better. I snap on my headphones and step onto the sand. I find the yucca plant with the orange flower and stand perpendicular to it. I flick the ON switch and Ruva lights up.

This is where I belong.

The south side of the cove is shady and cooler. I start there.

1 2 3 4 5

Nothing.

6 7 8 9

I move ten paces to my left.

10 11 12 13

Nothing. *Don't panic.* It's got to be here.

I move closer to the water and Ruva starts to beep. The Unattainable Find! I grab my sifter and shovel. I dig and dig.

Brain says: Congratulations. A quarter.

I rinse it and shove it into my pocket. Once, Minny and I

found a sandwich bag full of pennies—probably some little kid's life savings. We counted out the change and bought a chocolate-covered frozen banana to share at the Beach Shack.

Why'd Minny have to move? My one safe person dragged away. Just how Cat's Cove pulls everything back into the sea. The current sucks everything it touches to the bottom and swirls it around like a gigantic drain.

I think about what Dad said today. Was Minny a forced friend? No. She was real.

Brain says: How do you know?

My heart bumps.

Ruva beeps again.

I dig. It's a pacifier attached to a metal ring. Last year, I found a high heel, a baby bottle, and an empty carton of wine.

Brain says: That's just a bad babysitter.

I scan the horizon. The waves are calm, the current mellow. Maybe I was standing closer to the yuccas on the hill?

"Hellllooooo!"

I jump.

Patrick. His hair sways, his skin golden in the disappearing sunlight.

"I *knew* you'd be down here! I thought to myself, I bet Cora's at the cove, because that's where I saw her last time." He leans over to catch his breath. "Do you come here every day?"

Brain says: Is there no peace in this world?

My face feels hot. I consider ignoring him, but finally I pull off my headphones. "You scared me."

"Sorry. It's just, I ran the whole way here. I'm actually really fast."

Heat covers my entire body as I walk farther down the beach and hope Patrick takes a hint. Instead he follows me with his weird crown thing. "I have tests to run. Do you want to help?" His dark hair is electric; a halo of curls moves in the breeze.

"Patrick, you don't *have* to be my friend when we're not at school."

He considers this. "Most friends hang out after school. Don't you want a new friend?"

Brain says: Tell him to hit the road.

Instead, I shrug. "Whatever." The heat from my face begins to fade. My heartbeat calms.

"What are you looking for?"

Brain says: Don't tell him.

"Anything I find interesting," I say. The boulder on the hill looks sort of familiar. This might be where I was. I slip my headphones back on and methodically scan the sand.

Patrick follows. "How do you know when you've found it? How much did all that gear cost? How long have you been a treasure hunter?"

Brain says: I think you have a nonstop talker.

And just when I'm about to tell him to leave, Ruva begins to beep. I kneel and dig with my sifter.

For once Patrick doesn't say a word but kneels in the wet sand and digs with me. Our fingers bump into each other.

"I feel something," he says. "Right here."

I feel it too.

Patrick digs a huge gob of sand away as the water tries to suck the lost thing back down. Together we scrape until—it pops to the surface.

An old padlock.

I pick it up and rinse it off. It doesn't have a keyhole or a combination pad.

"Nice!" Patrick swipes at a big clump of wet sand running down the middle of his face with the back of his hand, but it just smears. Each time Patrick tries to wipe the sand away he makes it worse.

And then I begin to laugh.

Patrick smiles.

When I laugh, he does too. He sounds like a cross between a donkey and Santa Claus. He's somehow gotten sand all over his face.

I laugh harder.

Brain says: What's going on?

Tears run down our cheeks.

"Whew!" says Patrick. "You're funny."

No one's ever told me I'm funny before.

Brain says: I still don't get it.

We stop giggling, but the ghosts of our laughter hang in the air like clouds. I examine the treasure. The outside is rough, with what look like three tiny holes along the side. You can push the middle section in but only a little. I shake it. It sloshes, like water is trapped inside.

Brain says: This is something good.

"What is it?" asks Patrick.

I smile. "A treasure."

He nods, very serious. "I've always wanted to find one of those."

Brain says: What a dummy.

I wince. Brain usually thinks everyone's a dummy, even me, but there are dumber people than Patrick.

He squints. "What's that on the side? Can I see it?" He holds out his hand like he's waiting for me to bestow a precious gift upon him. You wouldn't expect that from the overzealous, sheepdog kind of boy that he is.

I place it gently in his hands.

"Amazing," he says.

"Look at these marks." On the right side there are three uniform scratch marks.

Patrick holds it up. "Maybe it's from outer space." A dribble of murky water runs down his arm.

Brain says: Is this guy for real?

He tries to pull the lock open like I did, but the seams are caked with mud. He hands it back to me.

"Or it could be from the plane crash." Immediately my face turns red.

Brain says: What did you do that for?

"The plane crash. You mean Catherine Van Larr?" Patrick's eyes dance, the wind moves his hair like it's keeping time with the waves.

I nod slightly.

"You're looking for clues?"

Brain says: Don't say it.

"The Cat's Treasure," I whisper-say.

He turns solemn. "A worthy goal."

The sun has long dipped into the sea, changing the sky from pink to hot pink with streaks of orange. Golden hour. In a few minutes everything will be dark.

"I have to go home," I say, pressing the lock to my chest.

He brushes the sand off his hands. "Me too, but that was amazing!" He pumps his hand into the air. "You're like a real live explorer—braving the mysteries of the deep to find treasure. Did you know scientists know less about the deepest part of the ocean than they do about outer space?" He stumbles on a rock and then rights himself. "See you at school tomorrow!"

Brain says: I can't believe you told him what you're looking for. Now he'll never leave us alone.

I put the treasure in my backpack and strap Ruva onto my bike.

Patrick gives me a salute and races up the embankment, not even bothering to use the trail, as he disappears behind the mass of aloe vera plants.

Brain says: Good riddance.

Yeah, good riddance. But for a moment it feels nice to have someone on my side again. Someone other than Brain.

CHAPTER 19

15 Minutes and 45 Seconds Until the Best and the Bad

It's five o'clock when I get home. Quickly, I stash my bike and Ruva in the garage. I'm bursting with news. I have to tell someone.

I text Minny: `I found something!!!`

Minny texts: `I have to get off my phone Moms` 🙁

I text: `Something important!!!`

Minny texts: `gtg`

"Cora, is that you?" Mom waits for me in the living room.

The new treasure in my backpack feels delicious. I'm as light as a puff of dandelion seed. Dad's going to freak. "Is Dad back?" I ask, breathless.

"No." Mom's perched on our living room couch, surrounded by pillows, her purse strap around her shoulders. "Did you have a good day?"

"Awesome."

She looks up from her phone, surprised. "Really, school

was good? Dad said you were at Custom Ride. What happened with Patrick? Was he nice?"

Oh right, school. I hesitate.

Brain says: Don't tell her about the treasure.

I say, "Yeah, he was all right."

"Wow, Cora. You're making great strides. Way to take the bull by the horns."

Ugh.

"I found something." I say and wait.

Brain says: Nooo.

Mom's distracted. "What?"

"At the cove."

"Uh-huh," she says. She finishes her text and looks up at me. "Did you feel anxious today?"

Brain says: Anxiety is a way of life.

I hesitate again. "I was okay."

"If it's too much work, why don't you come straight home from school instead of stopping at Custom Ride? Then you'll have more time for homework."

"No, I like helping Dad. It's fine."

"And what about the cove? You don't need to spend all your time there."

"Mom, I need the cove."

She lets out a large puff of air. "I can't win with you. Did you get the text I sent or the one from Aunt Janet?"

I shake my head.

She stands and brushes imaginary lint off her slacks.

"They messed up our spring order at The Little Boy Blue,

so now Aunt Janet and I have to go through the shipment piece by piece to straighten it out. Blue's here playing with Sunshine, so—do you think you could keep an eye on them?"

I slump onto the sofa. "Mommmm, no." I can't babysit tonight. I need to scroll through all my usual blogs about The Cat to look for clues. I have to examine the padlock and those weird scratch marks. I lie. "Dad was going to help me with a school project tonight."

Brain says: You're getting good at that.

"You can still do your project. Sunshine and Blue are watching TV in the den. It'll be just for an hour, tops." She feels my forehead. "What's wrong? You babysit them all the time."

I pull away. "I don't know. I'm too—"

Mom looks at me like I'm speaking alien. "You're too what?" Her phone dings. "Should I call Dr. Rosenthal?"

"No, Mom."

"Are you sure?"

"I don't even like her that much. Can't I get a different therapist?"

Mom gives me an exasperated look, then her phone dings again. She answers a text message and says absently, "Dr. Rosenthal is the best."

Sunshine and Blue laugh from the other room.

Brain says: There's no way you can babysit those brats.

But Dr. Rosenthal did say last week, just because I think something, doesn't mean it's true. She says I can control my anxiety. I can control my thoughts.

Brain says: Not likely.

117

"Fine," I say to Mom. "I'll watch them."

"You're the best, Cor." She heads for the door. "I've ordered pizza. It should be here in half an hour. Thank you, my perfect little soldier!" The door slams behind her.

I take off my backpack.

It's fine. I'm fine.

Blue and Sunshine can be easy, if they're getting along.

Chevy comes and sits on my lap. I doubt proper soldiers let dogs sit on their laps. He weighs 28 pounds. I rub the back of his head and he turns and gives me a doggy smile with his tongue hanging out. My heart begins to calm. I do love my Chevy dog.

Blue turns the corner. "Cora!" He gives me a giant hug and scratches Chevy's ears. "Want to play Legos?"

Chevy licks Blue's face. "He slimed me." He wipes off his cheek.

"Okay," I say. "Let's all play Legos."

"She said yes!" he yells to Sunshine, who drags a box almost as big as she is into the room. Once they're busy with Legos, I can examine the treasure. They dump the huge tub in front of me as a rainbow of plastic blocks clatter to the ground.

See, everything's fine.

We dig in and build. Blue's favorite thing right now is zombies, so I build him one.

"Use these ones," he says, shoving some neon-green blocks over to me. "They glow in the dark. They're scary."

"You like scary stuff, huh, Blue?"

"I do too," says Sunshine.

"Yeah, right. Like when Chevy sleeps in your room at night and scares you with his snoring."

Sunshine gives a very exaggerated eye roll, which I have never seen her do before. "He makes zombie noises in his sleep."

"Zombie noises are awesome." Blue growls and rolls his eyes into the back of his eye sockets so you can only see the white. He reaches for Sunshine.

She screams, "You're gross!"

"Plus I have my lightsaber." He pulls out his lightsaber, which he's hooked through his belt loop. He swings it at my face.

"Okay, okay," I say. "Watch where you swing that thing." He nearly misses smacking Sunshine full in the throat.

"Fine." Blue tucks the lightsaber back into his belt loop—it sticks out and keeps knocking over the zombie robots we've built. He and Sunshine crawl around looking for Lego pieces. While they're busy, I grab my backpack and make my way through the kitchen to the garage.

"Where are you going?" demands Sunshine.

"Nowhere."

"What's behind your back?"

"Nothing. I'm just getting something in the garage. I'll be back in a second."

I grab the air compressor in Dad's workshop to blow out the sand in the lock so I can get a better look.

"Cora!" says Blue, right behind me. "I thought you were playing with us."

Brain says: Buzz off, kid.

"I am," I say. "I'm just trying to do something really quick."

"I'm hungry."

"Mom ordered pizza. It should be here soon."

He shakes his head. "I'm hungry now."

"What's that?" Sunshine appears by his side.

"Nothing. Come on, let's play robot war while we wait for the pizza," I say as I head toward the Legos.

"No!" they both say in unison—they smile widely at each other. They know they're stronger together.

Brain says: Tiny minions.

I follow them to the fridge. "You can eat something small, but don't spoil your dinner." I sound like Mom.

"I want ice cream," Blue says, swinging the freezer open.

"Me too!"

"How about cereal?" I grab a box of Fruity O's and set it on the counter.

They look at each other again. "Ice cream," says Blue.

"Cereal's okay," my sister says.

Blue nods. "Okay, but I want to pour it myself."

"Yeah. Me too."

He scrambles onto the kitchen counter.

"How come Blue gets to climb on the counters and I don't?"

"He doesn't. Blue, don't climb up there. I'll get the bowl," I say, wrapping my hand around his wrist.

He ignores me and places his foot against the wall to boost himself higher, stretching to reach the bowls on the top shelf.

"Blue, get down. I'll get it."

Brain says: We should be examining treasure, not dealing with bratty kids.

Blue pushes me away. "No."

He stretches higher, placing his other foot on top of the toaster.

"Blue, stop!"

In one point five seconds, he slips.

I reach for him. But he falls and hits the floor with a loud pop.

"Blue!"

His lightsaber dangles from the handle in the cupboard door, his belt loop ripped from his pants. He sits up, dazed—his eyes glassy. He lifts his arm; it's strangely bent.

Brain says: That doesn't look right.

Blue lets out a wail. "My arm!"

He and Sunshine both begin to cry.

My legs turn to jelly. It's so hot in here. I slink against the cupboards to the floor. I can't breathe. "Blue, it's okay," I say between shallow breaths.

He continues to cry.

"Don't. Move." I have to do something. I *am* the baby-sitter. Dr. Rosenthal says a panic attack is nothing more than unfounded fear.

Brain says: Fear is fear.

Blue cradles his arm in his lap.

"Cora, help," says Sunshine. She pulls on my arm. And I want to help, but a gigantic hand wraps itself around my lungs and squeezes out every inch of air. I close my eyes. I do deep breathing, but it feels like my lungs have been sucked dry. "It's okay," I whisper-say to Blue. At least I think I say it. I hope I say it.

Blue wails, his face red and sweaty.

"Call Mom," I tell Sunshine between breaths.

She runs to the phone.

But then the front door opens and Mom stands there. "I left my cell phone. What's wrong?" Aunt Janet rushes into the kitchen behind her and scoops up Blue, then she sees his crooked arm.

"Sunshine, what happened?" asks Mom.

"He fell."

"No, Cora pulled me off the counter." Tears stream down Blue's face. He really believes it—he thinks I did this to him.

"No," I say.

What kind of person can't help someone they love so much?

Mom kneels beside me. "Breathe," she says. "You're okay." She wraps her arms around me, pulling me partially onto her lap. She hasn't held me like this since I was little.

"Blue slipped right off the counter," my sister says. "He slipped like when they step on a banana in a cartoon." But she doesn't laugh.

With Blue in her arms, Aunt Janet heads to the front door. "We're going to the emergency room. I'll call you later."

"Okay." Mom nods.

"Can you stand, Cora? What do you need?" she asks.

I try to squish the panic back into place in my brain. My fingers inch along the tile floor and feel for the chipped piece. If I can just find Australia, then everything will be okay.

Sunshine stands in our empty doorway and stares after Blue. "What's going to happen to him?"

Mom doesn't answer. Instead she rocks me back and forth. "You're all right."

I nod, but I know I'm not. Another lie.

Mom presses a button on her phone—waits—then, "I'd like to make an appointment with Dr. Rosenthal. Yes, it's urgent."

Sunshine grabs the back of Mom's shirt and holds on to her like a baby koala, her big eyes glossy with tears. "Are you okay, Cora?"

Breathe. Breathe. Breathe.

Even though I hate it, and I know Brain hates it, I cry. I'm a monster—not even a real person.

Mom's arm curls around me as she pats my back.

Slowly, I catch my breath. "How come I'm not getting better?" My body aches with knowing that I can't help anyone, not even myself.

Mom's hand makes little circles across my back. "I don't know."

Brain says: No one understands you but me.

CHAPTER 20

Wednesday: 10 Minutes and 13 Seconds Until I Know the Truth about Me

*T*he carpet under Dr. Rosenthal's door is thin—pressed flat by hundreds of feet that have passed through her office. The waiting room has six chairs, one couch, and one fish tank, which usually has ten tropical fish, but today there are only nine.

"What happened to number ten?" I ask.

Mom looks up from her phone. "What?"

"There used to be ten."

"I have no idea what you're talking about." She goes back to her phone and texts Dad furiously. He was supposed to pick up Sunshine but at the last minute, he said he couldn't and blamed Custom Ride. I blame Uncle Richie.

Brain says: You know what happened to that fish.

Dead. Flushed down the toilet bowl.

Sigh.

Doctor Rosenthal sees patients like me, with and without talking brains, on Mondays, Tuesdays, and Wednesdays. If there's an emergency, you can call her cell. Today's visit is an emergency, but it's also Wednesday and there was an opening, so there's no special emergency fee.

Don't believe for a second that I haven't heard Mom and Dad talk about how expensive Dr. Rosenthal is or how this is my second emergency visit.

I text Minny: Had a bad day. I miss you.

Surprisingly, she texts me right back.

Minny: Sorry Ive been MIA I strted school it ws good but I misssss la quinta beach

Me: Blue broke his arm. I had another panic attack.

Minny: Oh noooo

Me: Do you think you'll ever move back?

"Cora," says the lady at the front desk.

I look up.

Mom stands. "Put your phone away, Cora."

Minny: Mybe

Me: When?

Minny: IDK r u sitting w Jocelyn at lunch

Jocelyn with the googly eyes?

Me: No.

Minny: u need 2 mke new friends

But Minny's my friend.

I don't text her back. If making friends were easy, then I'd do it already.

Brain says: You don't need forced friends. You have me.

"Cora," says Mom. "Come on."

Dr. Rosenthal comes out to greet us.

"Aren't you coming with me?" I hold on to Mom's hand.

She shakes her head. "You did fine without me last time."

"She did," says Dr. Rosenthal, smiling at me. "Come on in, Cora. Your mom will be waiting right here when we're done."

I turn off my phone and follow Dr. Rosenthal into the office. It has couches with fuzzy pillows and fruity candles on a little table in the center of the room. I sit in what has become my regular seat.

Dr. Rosenthal smiles. I think the smile and fuzzy pillows are supposed to say you're safe in this office.

Brain says: Nothing's ever safe.

Dr. Rosenthal interrupts my thoughts. "Your mother filled me in on what happened last night while you were babysitting, but I'd like to hear about it from your point of view."

"Okay," I say.

"Is Brain talking to you right now?"

Brain says: Don't you even.

She writes something in her notebook, which is probably stuffed full of bad things about me.

Brain says: And me.

Dr. Rosenthal pats the cushion next to her. "How about we ask Brain to sit here next to us and join our conversation?"

"Brains don't sit on sofas."

She squints and taps her chin. "You're right, of course. I just think it's important that we invite Brain to the conversation since he's become such a large part of your life lately. Your negative self-talk seems to be increasing, especially since Minny moved."

Brain says: Listen, lady. I've been here since always.

I can't remember a time without Brain. Sometimes he's louder than others, but he's always there. Some days I have no choice but to listen to him.

I adjust the pink fluffy pillow at my elbow. "He's always in my head."

Dr. Rosenthal nods. "Your mom said that you didn't always talk about Brain. But now these thoughts have become more intrusive. Last session you said he seemed, to use a direct quote, to be 'bossier.' Do you still feel that's true?"

I nod.

"Sometimes people name the anxious voice in their head. It's very normal. You call that voice Brain, but it's just your voice, your own negative thoughts."

She continues, "But you don't have to listen to those thoughts."

Brain says: Dr. Rosenthal knows nothing.

My heart thrums.

"Tell me what happened when you were babysitting." Dr. Rosenthal seems like she wants to help, but this is what I've been trying *not* to think about. I can't get the image of Blue lying on the floor with his arm bent back out of my mind. My stomach twists.

Brain says: It's all your fault.

This morning, Aunt Janet called and said Blue had a severe fracture and they had to do surgery.

Brain says: Still your fault.

I can't get the noise out of my head.

Brain says: CRACK.

And the crying.

Brain says: The worst.

And his face.

Brain says: Snot galore.

What if Aunt Janet never trusts me again?

Brain says: She won't.

What if Blue hates me?

Brain says: He does.

What if I never get better?

Brain says: Get better from what?

Dr. Rosenthal sets out a box of tissues. "You seem to have a lot on your mind." She says that a lot.

The lump in my throat grows. My voice box has decided to go on a trip. Maybe my voice box and Brain should go on vacation together. Finally, I manage, "I'm a bad person."

Dr. Rosenthal shakes her head no. "You worry a lot, but that doesn't make you bad. Panic attacks are just the body's way of dealing with unresolved stress—"

"But I love Blue. Why couldn't I help him?"

"It has nothing to do with love, Cora," Dr. Rosenthal says. "When you're in a stressful situation, your brain shouts high alert and so does your body."

Brain says: I'm the best friend you ever had.

"We've got to transform the stress you feel into something productive."

I'm trying.

"How are your affirmations going?" Dr. Rosenthal asks.

That stupid box. I shrug.

"You know, Cora, you don't have to believe every thought you have. Just because you think it, doesn't mean it's true."

But Brain's just Brain. I haven't ever thought of him as anything other than me. Brain tells the truth. Brain keeps me safe. Brain alerts me to danger, human or otherwise.

"Thoughts are just that—passing ideas. They are not *you*." Dr Rosenthal looks so earnest that I almost believe her.

Brain says: You can't survive without me.

"Were you hungry, angry, lonely, tired, or stressed yesterday?"

The treasure in my bag was a happy thing. But then I had to babysit, which normally I don't mind, but since Minny left everything feels like too much.

"I've got a list of ways to help manage your stress," Dr. Rosenthal says. She goes through the list, telling me how to pay attention to particular triggers. When she's finished, she stands. "Just remember you are in charge of your brain, Cora. Friends are *very* important."

I nod. I'm horrible at making friends.

Brain says: Making friends is impossible.

She opens the door and I follow her out into the waiting room.

Mom smiles and stands. "How'd it go?"

"Great," says the doctor.

Mom gives me the side-eye.

I shrug.

She hands me her keys. "Why don't you wait in the car? I want to talk to Dr. Rosenthal for a second."

Brain says: So she can get the bad report.

Mom and Dr. Rosenthal lean their heads close together; their voices hush.

I take the keys and push the door halfway open, but I pause over the threshold.

Mom says, "I worry about putting her on medication."

Dr. Rosenthal says, "Behavior therapy can only do so much. I hope you and your husband will consider the combination of therapy and medicine. It could really help—"

"Cora." Mom cranes her neck and spies me standing halfway in the doorway. "I told you to wait in the car."

"Okay."

A few minutes later in the car, Mom says, "That was good, right?"

The bowling ball in my stomach sloshes. "Do I have to take medicine?"

Mom sucks in her breath as she pulls out of the parking garage. "Did you hear us talking about that? Dad and I aren't sure that's the bridge we want to cross. I still think some good, old-fashioned elbow grease will do the trick."

I pick at my fingernails.

"You don't want medicine, do you?" Mom asks.

Brain says: Medicine is for sick people.

I hesitate, then shake my head no.

Mom sighs like she's relieved. "Well, good. Why don't we swing by Aunt Janet's to check on Blue?"

"Mom, no."

"But Blue wants to see you."

Brain says: Doubtful.

I do deep breathing.

I text Minny: `I'm a monster.`

Minny texts: `Sometimes we all feel that way`

Brain says: Sometimes it's true.

CHAPTER 21

4 Minutes and 11 Seconds Until Blue Knows the Truth

*B*lue won't look at me. He lies on the couch in Aunt Janet's living room watching cartoon zombies, his arm wrapped in a fiberglass cast with a waterproof liner so he can get it wet. Pillows are placed carefully around him, so he won't break again.

"Didn't they have blue casts?" I ask.

Aunt Janet grimaces. "They were out of blue, but that's okay, right, Blue? Green is your second-favorite color."

"So what." Blue pushes a car along his cast and then sets it flying into the air. It drops and clatters to the floor.

Mom announces, "Blue, we get what we get and we don't throw a fit."

Brain says: That's so Mom.

Even Aunt Janet gives her the side-eye.

I pick up the car and drive it along his leg, but he shakes it off. "Blue, I'm sorry," I say. "I'm sorry I couldn't." My voice catches. "Help you."

He won't look at me.

Aunt Janet gives me a tired smile.

I try again. "I'm sorry you fell."

Brain says: I think he should apologize to you.

"The next time I babysit, I promise it'll be better."

He looks up—his eyebrows squinch together. "I don't want you to babysit me *ever again!*" He throws another car across the living room.

It's like I've been slapped.

Aunt Janet pats his leg. "Okay, buddy, that's enough. It was an accident, you know that." She turns to Mom. "I think it's best if we take a break for a while. The doctor says Blue needs his rest, and you could use some time so Cora can focus on getting better too."

My eyes sting. I blink fast, willing my tears back, because that would be too humiliating.

She puts her hand on my shoulder. "I'm sorry, Cora. You know we love you—Blue just needs a little time."

Brain says: Don't let her see you cry.

Mom folds her arms. "Janet, I don't think that's necessary. Cora's getting the help she needs. Right, honey?" She pats my leg.

Aunt Janet looks away. The room is silent except for the TV. It's true, then. I'm a monster and even Aunt Janet can see it.

"Let's discuss this later, okay?" Aunt Janet says, her voice tight. "Blue's tired."

Blue covers his eyes with his forearm. The sun from the window spotlights him, his cast glowing green.

"But—" Mom begins.

"June, I seriously don't want to talk about this in front of the kids. I'll call you later. And you need to have that conversation with Cora, *the one we talked about*." Aunt Janet tucks the blanket around Blue. He kicks it off.

Mom's look is dangerous.

Aunt Janet walks us to the front door and grabs the handle. She turns to me. "Cora, we just want you to get better, and that might take a little time."

Mom's face is pinched. "This is ridiculous."

Now my aunt folds her arms across her chest. "Get it sorted, June."

In one point five seconds, Mom and I are standing on the doorstep. The door closes with a definitive snap. The bougainvillea vine shudders.

Can you sort someone like me?

Mom marches to the car and flings the door open, muttering to herself. "Perfect timing, Janet. Just perfect."

Without making a sound, I slide into my seat. Mom drives us home in six minutes and four seconds.

At home, Dad sits in the kitchen, scrolling through his phone. "How was therapy?" he asks. He looks almost happy.

"Fine," I say.

"Fine," says Mom.

The air hangs heavy with us being kicked out of Aunt Janet's house.

"Did Dr. Rosenthal suggest medicine again?" he asks.

Mom doesn't meet his eyes. "I think there's something

about it on the papers she gave me. But I don't know if Cora's quite there yet."

Dad's eyebrows raise and he looks at me. "Really?"

I examine the basket of clementines on the kitchen counter. Now Mom's lying to Dad?

She gives him a pointed look. "We can discuss this later." She sets her purse down with a thunk, like that's the end of that conversation.

Dad asks me, "How're you feeling? Is Dr. Rosenthal helping?"

I shrug.

"She came very highly recommended," Mom says.

I sit at the kitchen island and take an orange from the basket, peeling it slowly.

"She's okay."

"And expensive," says Mom. "When you're expensive, you're the best."

Dad changes the subject. "If you're wondering about the new rehab, it looks really awesome. They're doing all these innovative things that help their patients stay motivated. Richie seemed really good. Better than I expected." He smiles. The wrinkles around his eyes crinkle.

Mom scoffs. "I've heard that before. We'll see how long it lasts." She tosses the car keys onto the table.

I jump.

"Why do you always bring that up? It was eleven years ago. When are you going to let it go?" Dad glares at her.

"What?" I ask.

But neither of them acknowledges me.

"What happened?" I set the peeled orange on the counter.

Mom rifles through her purse to find her phone.

Dad storms off to his room.

Mom marches into the den.

The bowling ball in my stomach feels heavier.

Chevy and I go to my room. I lie on my bed and stretch my limbs across the mattress—splayed like a starfish. I imagine myself floating down, down, to the bottom of the sea. I can almost feel the current rocking me. I take a deep breath.

1 2 3 4 5

I may never get up.

The padlock sits in my backpack. What difference does it make if I find The Unattainable Find? I still can't help being me.

CHAPTER 22

38 Minutes Until I'm the Level Head

That night Sunshine crawls into bed with me. Her warm body settles next to mine, and normally I don't like when she climbs in and takes up the whole mattress and tangles up my covers. But tonight, I don't mind.

I can't sleep either.

Brain says: Speak for yourself.

"What's wrong?" I ask.

"I had a bad dream."

I put my arm around her and trace her hand with my finger. She smells like sleep and outside.

"About what?"

"A tsunami swallowed our house and our family." There are tears in her voice. She scoots closer.

"That's not going to happen."

"How do you know?"

Brain says: Northern California had a tsunami after an earthquake in Alaska.

"We're not anywhere near Alaska."

Sunshine turns. Her bright eyes reflect the light from the moon. "What happens in Alaska?"

"They get all the big earthquakes that stir up waves and cause tsunamis. But down here in La Quinta Beach, we're safe."

Brain says: Safety is relative.

Hush, Brain. No one scares Sunshine.

Sunshine nods, but her eyebrows knit together like an invisible thread has pulled them tight. "But what if there's a big earthquake in La Quinta Bay?" She clasps her hands together under her chin.

"There won't be."

"But how do you *know*?"

Sunshine's never like this. I pull her hand into mine. Dr. Rosenthal says when I get worried, I should focus on facts—the truth. I take a deep breath. "Okay, I don't know for sure, but it's *unlikely* there'll be an earthquake here. It probably won't happen. And if it does, I'll keep you safe." I hesitate. "And Mom and Dad too. We have that fishing boat, right? We can get in that."

She tucks my comforter under her chin and stares into the dark. "Okay." I feel her body relax a little.

I count her breaths.

1 2 3

"What about Blue's arm?" she asks, her voice quieter now. "Will he be able to play with me again, just like before?"

"Yes, the doctors know how to fix him. He'll be just like new."

She nods, her head bumping into mine. "All right." Her breathing slows. "And Cora, what about you?"

My heart quickens.

"Are you going to be okay again? Can you still be our babysitter?"

My stomach knots.

Brain says: Lie.

But I can't. Not to Sunshine. I pick at a loose thread from my blanket. "I don't know."

"You will be," she says as she curls up on her side. She yawns. "Will you do affirmations with me?"

Ugh. Affirmations. But for Sunshine—

"Okay."

"You start," she says.

I take a deep breath. Mom's cursive writing appears in my brain. I say, "I can do hard things." I wait.

Sunshine's silent.

I jostle her a little with my elbow. "You have to say it with me."

She sighs.

1 2 3 4

She's asleep.

I turn on my side to face her and breathe in the dark. "I don't know if I can do hard things."

The night envelops us. Sunshine and I float in outer

space—our stars bump into each other, hers bright, mine dim—searching for the same orbit.

"I don't know if I can," I repeat.

Brain says: You can't.

CHAPTER 23

Thursday: 7 Minutes and 9 Seconds Until
I Am High-Fived to Death

School this morning feels even more uncomfortable now that I have a clear picture of who I really am.

Brain says: Monsters shouldn't have to go to school.

I'm too tired to be in Patrick's orbit.

It's block day so I only have three classes today. Biology is first. My feet drag as I follow him—my backpack heavier than ever. I am a human tomato, but my hoodie's safely in place to deflect unwanted stares.

Patrick bounces ahead with his electric hair and toothy smile. "Hellooo!" He holds up his hand. "Lupe, high five!" He's the self-appointed best friend of every person at Las Olas Middle School.

Lupe ignores him.

"That's okay, next time." His smile is undeterred. "High five," he says to an unsuspecting girl. She slaps it.

"Yes!" He pumps his fist in the air.

Brain says: That's high five number seven.

I give Patrick a weak smile.

Mr. Camacho walks by and slaps Patrick's never-ending raised hand. "When are you coming to help me organize the lab?"

"Soon, soon," says Patrick.

Brain says: Number eight.

"My main man," says a kid with crutches. "How's outer space?"

"Still there."

I stop to tie my shoe, but Patrick waits for me.

A sea of kids part. "Why weren't you at STEAM?" a red-headed girl, twice my size, calls out to Patrick. She slams her locker door.

"Sorry, Natasha. I've got a super-important assignment right now. No time for extracurriculars." Patrick holds up his hand.

She doesn't slap it. "Who's this?" she asks, pointing at me.

"Cora Altman."

Natasha appraises me.

My body's on fire; I feel rocket red.

"I like your kicks," she says, looking at my feet.

I swallow but can't respond.

Natasha gives Patrick a half-hearted high five to his ever-waiting hand.

Brain says: Number nine.

"Whatever. Yeah, too busy," she says. "But you're way behind."

"You're only as behind as you feel," Patrick yells after her. He smiles at me and holds up his hand.

Without thinking, I slap it.

"Yes!" he says. "I got a Cora-five!" He dances down the hallway as his key chains clack together, creating his own Patrick soundtrack.

Brain says: Number ten.

Ugh.

In between saying hi to everyone who passes us, Patrick feeds me information about outer space as we make our way to biology.

"Did you know a NASA space suit costs two hundred and fifty million dollars?"

"Did you know there's evidence that there's life on Mars?"

"Did you know Halley's Comet won't pass Earth again until 2061?"

Patrick barely takes a breath as facts shoot from his mouth. "When I graduate, I'm either going to live in Cape Canaveral at NASA, or if there are people living on the moon by then, of course, I'll live there," he says as if it's the most natural thing.

Mr. Farns stands in his classroom doorway as we pass. "Hello, Miss Altman. Any news about my son's car? I called your dad, but he hasn't gotten back to me yet."

I splutter and shake my head.

"I like your hair today, Patrick," says Penny, a girl from my old elementary school. "It's very Einstein-esque." Patrick's hair is especially gigantic today.

Penny's friend rolls her eyes.

"Thanks, Penny. I'll take that as a compliment."

My head spins. How does he remember everyone's name?

He turns to me. "I've saved money toward buying a seat on the Virgin Atlantic space flight. Soon, anyone who can afford a ticket can go."

"How much?" I ask.

He beams, since it's the first question I've asked him. "It's two hundred and fifty thousand dollars per ticket. Right now, I have six hundred and ninety-one dollars." He tries to look modest, but I can tell he's proud. "I'm almost there. I help my grandma with bingo. They do it every Friday and Saturday. I get eight dollars an hour *and* I get to eat all the desserts I want. Those are the perks of being related to Queen Bea."

I'm so tired. We stand in the doorway of my biology classroom.

"You're going to be late for class," I say.

But he just stands there. "Don't worry. Principal Shurtzer gave me this hall pass, so if I'm a little late, it's okay." He holds his hand up for another high five.

Brain says: He's being your forced friend for a hall pass?

I picture Minny's face. Forced friend?

"Cora, you should come over to my house after school," he says.

I can't go to the house of someone I barely know. Plus, what if I have another panic attack?

He lowers his voice. "I've got to show you something really, really important. It's going to blow your mind."

Brain says: I'd rather not.

"After school, I usually babysit," I say. But I know today that won't be true. Blue's cast and Aunt Janet's disappointed face flash before my eyes.

Ando and his pack walk toward us.

"Helloooo." Patrick holds up his hand for a high five.

My body tenses, waiting for their stares. My hoodie deflects them. *Pow. Pow. Pow.* My heart beats like it has wings, flapping in milliseconds.

The pack ignores Patrick, but Ando says, "My man." He slaps Patrick's hand.

Brain says: Number eleven.

Patrick laughs, loud and goofy.

Two boys in Ando's pack imitate it. But Ando ignores them. "How's your grandma?"

"Queen Bea? Excellent. Thank you for asking," he says. I don't think I'll ever get used to Patrick's too-loud voice.

I peek at Ando's face, but he's smiling at Patrick in earnest.

I take a step away from them and slip into biology.

Mr. Kim isn't here yet. The table where Minny and I usually sit is empty. Johnny, Sariah, Temple, and Jocelyn usually sit here too. Minny's friends with all of them; she was our glue.

Jocelyn sets her backpack on top of my table. She raises her eyebrows, making her forehead all wrinkled. Her gigantic eyes protrude out of her head.

Brain says: Is there a way we can shove those back in?

I ignore her bulging eyeballs and arrange my face into what I hope is a friendly expression.

"So, where's everyone?" she asks. The right side of her nose wrinkles like she's smelling low tide.

I shrug my shoulders up to my ears.

"Did Minny really move already?" Jocelyn's been absent this past week. "I thought it was next week."

I nod. Minny was supposed to move next week, but her mom's work changed the date.

Jocelyn sits on the stool for a moment and then stands up, quickly scanning the room. "Johnny!" she calls, waving.

I turn.

Johnny and Sariah are sitting at another table, near the cabinet with the beakers and experiment equipment.

"Guess I've got to go," she says, squeezing past me and sliding in between Johnny and Sariah like peanut butter and jelly. They erupt into giggles.

Mr. Kim bustles through the door with a box of empty jars. "All right, class. Sorry I'm late. We're getting ready for our unit on mollusks." He sets the box on the front counter.

The class quiets.

His gaze falls upon me, eyeing the empty table. "Where's Table Six?"

I trace the cracks in the wood with my index finger. The silence hurts my ears.

Mr. Kim grabs the seating chart. "Johnny, Sariah, Jocelyn, Temple, Minny, Cora." He looks up and spies Johnny. "Take your seat, please."

Johnny drags himself over and drops his bag on top of the table. He sits on the opposite side, sighing loudly, as he lays his head on his backpack like a pillow.

"Minny moved," someone says.

"That's right," says Mr. Kim. "How's she doing, Cora?"

As if on command, my face burns. I manage a stifled, "Fine."

Mr. Kim nods. "Very good."

He reads from the seating chart. "Sariah, Jocelyn, Temple, take your seats."

There are groans.

"You picked them. We'll make a change at the end of term, around Thanksgiving."

Jocelyn and Sariah slowly get up and place their backpacks gingerly on the table, next to Johnny's.

Sariah says, "Temple's absent."

"That's fine." Mr. Kim scoots the box of jars across the counter—they clank against each other. The clatter is just loud enough so that only Table Six can hear Johnny as he lifts his head. "If you're going to freak out again, do it over there." He points toward the door. "I don't want throw up on me."

Brain says: You didn't vomit.

Jocelyn rolls her big, fat eyeballs.

Sariah hisses, "Johnny." Then she manages a weak smile at me but won't hold eye contact for longer than two seconds.

Mr. Kim goes on about squids and dissection instructions.

I can't believe I'm saying this, but I wish Patrick were here.

CHAPTER 24

14 Minutes and 6 Seconds Until Patrick Reveals His Plan

*A*fter school, because I can't face Mom, or Aunt Janet, or Sunshine or Blue, I text Mom that I'm going to Patrick's house.

Brain says: Against my better judgment.

I text Minny: I'm going over to some kid's house.

Minny texts: Jocelyn tell her hi!!! <3 <3 <3

I text: No. Jocelyn's the worst.

Minny texts: shes alwys nice 2 me

My heart thumps. I take a deep breath.

I text: Must be easy when everyone's always nice to you.

I watch her text bubbles appear, but no words yet.

Patrick interrupts. "Come on!"

I slip my phone in my pocket. I don't want to see what she has to say.

Patrick's a few yards ahead. I can almost see the atoms

orbiting his head. His hair bounces as he jumps over a crack in the sidewalk. "Cora, you're going to die when you see what I got. Follow me."

It takes us exactly nine minutes to ride our bikes from school to Cascade Springs by the Sea, a trailer park perched on the top of a little hill with an ocean view. We stop and admire La Quinta Beach—the jetty is on the left with the harbor on the right. The reef made from sunken ships shimmers like gems under the surface of the ocean. The cove is hidden, but I know it's there.

"Did you bring the lock?" Patrick asks.

I shake my head. It's stuffed in the bottom of my sock drawer. I never did get to show Dad.

"Dang! I wanted to check it out again. I think it's something called an impossible lock."

The entrance sign of Cascade Springs by the Sea says NO CHILDREN ALLOWED. I immediately pull up my hoodie because—well—I am a child.

"You cold?" Patrick asks as he swings his leg over his bike and jumps off. "We have to walk our bikes in here. I know it's dumb, but the Homeowners Association says I have to. This is an adult-only place, but Grandma's on the board so they let me live here even though, technically, I'm a child. There are some perks to being Queen Bea's grandson." He smiles broadly.

An old man shuffles down the sidewalk.

"Hey there, Wally!" Patrick calls in his Patrick-sized voice.

Wally inches a walker past us. His shirt says *Go ahead, make my day*. His slippers trail frayed strips of green fabric, and they sound like he's sandpapering the sidewalk. He scowls at us and grumbles something under his breath.

"That's our neighbor. He walks a lot. I'm like his best friend," Patrick explains. "See ya later, Wally! Have a good one." He holds up his hand for a high five, which Wally ignores.

We head toward a light yellow mobile home with a sign on the door that says DON'T MESS WITH ME I'M THE BEA. The doormat is in the shape of a beehive. *BEE Sweet, Remove Your Shoes.* In the front yard, plastic bees the size of dinner plates are staked among the boulders and cactus. Classical music plays from next door.

"Is your grandma home?" I park my bike near a patch of gravel.

"I think so." Patrick points to the opposite side of the front yard. "Park over there. Marbella doesn't like anyone's stuff next to her property line."

The music gets louder. A lady in an apple-green, glittery tracksuit and dark hair steps onto the porch, her hands on her hips.

Patrick says, "Hellloooo, Ms. Marbella! Don't worry, I got it."

"You're a good boy, Patrick. You know the rules, my love." She blows him a kiss.

Patrick nods and walks my bike over five feet. "My grandma calls her a fusspot," he whispers.

I follow Patrick to the front door. He bellows through the screen, "Grandma! I'm home—I brought a friend from school—so don't worry—we're going to my room and then out to do research."

A tall woman, tanned and wrinkled, with hair perched high on top of her head like a beehive, appears in the doorway. "How many times have I told you to quit ordering things from the interwebs?" She shakes two packages at him and then sets them roughly on the floor. "I don't want you internet shopping. Where's my credit card?"

Patrick sputters, "I didn't—I'm sorry. Grandma, it's for the *greater good*." He adds, "I'll pay you back."

She gives him a withering look, her arms folded across her chest.

"I'm sorry, it's just . . ." His voice trails away.

"I know. I know. It's going to improve *all humanity*, or something like that." She pats him on the head, flattening his hair, and for a second, Patrick looks five years old.

She turns and smiles. "Hello, honeybee, how are you?"

Immediately my face burns. I look at my feet.

She holds out her hand. I think I'm supposed to shake it. "I'm Beatrice Ethel Borgwin. But you can call me Bea. Queen Bea." She points to the metal bees dangling from her ears. "Easy to remember, right?"

Patrick saves me. "This is my friend, Cora. My new *best* friend."

I shrink, a little.

I follow them inside, where every available space is filled with bees—yellow throw pillows, blankets, framed photos, figurines, beeswax candles, and more.

"Wow," I say.

"I'm what they call a bee connoisseur. If there's a bee on it, I have it. They're the most amazing insects." She holds out a little bee-shaped dish. "Huckleberry honey caramel?"

"Thank you," I mumble, trying to ignore the heat in my face. I pick up a gold-wrapped candy. The wrapper says *Bee-rrific*.

"I order them special from Queen Bee Farms, halfway across the United States." She turns to Patrick. "Speaking of ordering things—" She wags a finger at him. "Lay off my credit card."

He gives her a winning smile. "I'm sorry."

Immediately, he's forgiven. "Patty-boy has got a talent for making friends. Makes them everywhere he goes. Right, baby?" Queen Bea says.

Patrick beams.

"Just like my Joni, before she passed, God rest her soul." She places her hand over her heart like she's saying the Pledge of Allegiance.

Patrick nods solemnly. "My mom," he whispers as he picks up a framed photo of a lady with fair skin and dark hair sitting with a man with glasses and a uniform. He points at her. "This is my mom." Patrick's hair is the same—curly and wild—plus they have toothy smiles to match.

He then points to the man—his arm is wrapped around the lady. "And this is my dad." The man's smile is more serene, but I can see where Patrick gets his eyes, dark like the Challenger Deep, the most cavernous part of the ocean.

"They died when I was three." Patrick's eyes become even darker. No, sadder. He swallows hard as he wipes imaginary dust off the frame. "I don't remember them as much as I wish."

I nod. I think I understand. The wishing on stars and dandelions and buried treasure—always wanting what you don't have. That longing fills me up, and now I see it fills Patrick up too.

Brain says: You are nothing alike.

Queen Bea interrupts. "But we have the photo albums." She puts her arm around Patrick. "Lots and lots of photo albums. Patrick, they were the best people I ever knew or ever will."

Patrick places the frame back on the table and the whole feeling in the room has changed.

There's a seven-second pause, then she says, "What am I doing, going on and on? You two have better things to do than to sit and listen to me."

"Dad used to say it's always best to be polite," Patrick says.

"Yes, he did. Politest man I ever met." She pats his cheek. "And you're just like him. Like *both* of them—makes me proud just to hear you say it."

"They died in a scuba-diving accident."

Lost in the Challenger Deep?

Queen Bea shudders. "On vacation. It was a fluke. One in a million. I just think it was their time." She squeezes him a little tighter. "But at least I have you."

Patrick drops his head and the curls cover his eyes.

Queen Bea picks up the packages and hands them to him.

"Now, go clean your room while I make you two a snack. I've got to get down to the senior center. Something's wrong with the bingo cage."

Patrick smiles. His mood lifts to his previous altitude.

"Three Hot Pockets, please," he says.

"Three this time?" she asks, walking toward the kitchen. "Must have been a busy day."

"What about you?" he asks. "Do you want a Hot Pocket?"

I shake my head.

"Are you sure? We have pepperoni or just plain cheese."

I shake my head again.

He yells, "Make a plain cheese for Cora, just in case she changes her mind."

Brain says: There's no changing me.

"You betcha," yells Queen Bea from the kitchen. "I've got my microwaving finger all ready."

I follow Patrick down the hallway toward the only thing in the house that's not plastered with bees. Instead, his door is covered in planets, stars, galaxies—drawings of aliens and rockets, as well as articles about NASA.

"Do you believe in time travel?" he asks, opening the door.

I can almost see neurons zipping through his cranium. Does Patrick have a talking Brain like me?

Brain says: He's not *that* special.

"Like time machines and stuff?" I ask.

He nods, his face hopeful. He sets the packages on his bed, alongside twenty other boxes tossed in various degrees of peril all around his room.

"Uh, I don't know. Maybe."

"I knew it!" He pumps his fist into the air. "I just knew you'd get it. I can tell things about people and I just knew that you are someone who understands reason and logic."

Brain says: Reasonable and logical are not the words I'd use to describe him.

Patrick continues, "Einstein said if you can travel at the speed of light, then you can slow down time. If you can alter the earth's gravitational pull, you can bend it. It's the perfect recipe for a time traveler!" He spreads his arms out triumphantly like he's just solved every problem that ever existed. "Did you know there's a lunar eclipse happening next week?" He waits for me to respond.

The heat from my face slowly starts to fade. Gingerly, I sit on a pile of boxes. "Cool," I say.

"Don't you know what that means?!"

Normally, I hate feeling like I don't know the answers to questions. Normally, I hate people talking to me and expecting a response. Normally, I'd prefer to be home in my room with Chevy.

But I can't help but feel a little curious.

"Three times a year there's a lunar eclipse that changes the sun's gravitational pull. When that happens it theoretically bends time, which creates a wormhole to travel through." He climbs onto his bed. "And I'm building a time machine!" He leaps high into the air, then lands with a *BOOM* on the floor. The double-wide trailer shakes.

A moment later Queen Bea opens the door, balancing a

plate of Hot Pockets. "My stars, Patrick! What's going on in here? I've told you not to jump off the bed. It'll set the trailer loose." She clears a place on his desk and puts down the plate.

I imagine their trailer rolling off the cliff.

"Sorry," he says. "I tripped."

She surveys his room. "And I told you to clean up this mess."

"I know. I will, today. I promise."

"Where's my credit card?"

He grabs it from his desk and places it onto her open hand. "Your card, my lady." Patrick salutes her.

She laughs and flicks his hair.

At Minny's house, her mom was always working. At my house, Sunshine bugs me to death, but here at Patrick's, it feels different. Sort of comfy.

Queen Bea leaves the room. Patrick jumps on top of his bed and raises a box ceremoniously over his head. "I hereby declare that you, Cora Altman, will be my second-in-command."

Brain says: What's so great about being second?

He dumps out everything—papers, wires, rolls of cellophane, metal rings, boots, something that looks like a purple morph suit. It all piles at his feet. He's a lion ready to roar. "And I'll be *your* second!"

Brain says: You can't both be second.

He continues, "I'll be your right-hand man! I'll help you find The Cat's treasure, and you'll be my right-hand woman and help me be the first person ever to travel back in time!"

He jumps off the bed again and the floor shudders.

Queen Bea yells from the hallway, "Patrick!"

He smiles. "Our first order of business is to open these packages." He tosses one to me. "We need to hurry if we're going to have everything ready next week for the eclipse. Are you in?"

I stare at the yellow envelope in my lap.

Brain says: Don't do it.

My atoms vibrate. Patrick's smile is contagious.

I take a deep breath and rip it open.

CHAPTER 25

24 Minutes Until I Find a Clue

*M*inny texts me: `Not everyone likes me its hrd being new-Some pple r rude`

Jocelyn flashes in my mind. Then choir, and Mr. Farns's class, and lying on the ground on Friday with faces and eyeballs surrounding me. How the concrete felt like sandpaper and Nurse Celebran's bony fingers wrapped tightly around my wrist.

I know all about hard. And now Minny knows how it feels too.

Minny texts: `r u mad at me`

I stare at the screen.

I text: `No.`

I text: `I don't know`

Brain says: Except, you do.

After Patrick's house, when I get home, Dad and Uncle Richie are sitting on Grandma Altman's cushions looking at old photo albums, like everything's A-OK—like they do this all the time.

I hesitate in the doorway.

"Hey, Cor-Bell." Dad pats the seat next to him. "Come say hey to your uncle. He has a special pass to see family. You just missed Uncle Joaquin on Skype." He snaps the lid closed on his laptop.

Brain says: How come *he's* out?

I eye Uncle Richie warily. He certainly seems healthier than when I saw him on Saturday night.

Uncle Richie looks up from the photo album. His eyes are clear but red. He nods at me.

"The new facility thought it would be helpful for him to say hey to the family—to see some friendly faces." Dad smiles wide.

I nod. Except, where are Mom and Sunshine?

Now my uncle's face has more angles than curves.

Brain says: Rehab doesn't look good on him.

His hair's slicked back and he must be wearing Dad's clothes, because they're too big. Uncle Richie and Dad stare at me. I feel my face burn.

Dad clears his throat. "It's been a long time, Rich." He pats him on the back.

Uncle Richie twists the bottom of his shirt around his finger as a pink color crawls up his neck and spreads across his face. He mumbles, "It's been too long."

My heart bumps. Uncle Richie turns into a human tomato like me?

Brain says: Genetics are weird.

Why would he be embarrassed around me?

Politely, I nod. Although I have no idea how long it's been. The program from Grandma Vo's funeral last year sits on the coffee table. I pick it up. There she is, all young and beautiful on her wedding day. There she is, with her three little boys. There she is, with all her grandkids. Poor Vo. She would've loved to see her son again. Why didn't Uncle Richie come back until now?

"Where's Mom and Sunshine?" I ask, setting the program gently on the table.

"Store," says Dad. "Out of cereal or something." He glances at Uncle Richie, like he's trying to gauge if he believes it.

Uncle Richie holds the photo album carefully, like it's The Unattainable Find.

The silence is awkward.

1 2 3 4

Finally, Dad says, "Cora, go get that thing you found at Cat's Cove the other day. Mom told me about it. We'd love to see it, wouldn't we, Rich?"

My heart bumps.

Richie nods.

Dad, no.

Brain says: How dare he?

Treasure hunting is our father-daughter thing. Not even Mom or Sunshine come with us. It's definitely not for an uncle who I don't even remember.

My feet won't move.

Dad shifts so he speaks directly to Uncle Richie. "Cora and

I feel pretty certain The Cat's treasure will be somewhere near the cove. When you get another pass, I'll take you there. You won't believe how much it's changed."

Uncle Richie nods again.

"Go get it." Dad slaps his thighs like I'm Chevy.

My chest feels tight. I take a step toward my room and then, "It's at school," I say.

"Why'd you take it to school?"

I hesitate. "I wanted to show my, um, my friend."

Dad looks at his phone and his eyebrows shoot up. "Dang, Rich. We're going to be late! I've got to get you back before your time is up."

They hurry out through the garage and get into Dad's car. As they turn out of our driveway, Chevy whines.

I kneel and rub behind his ears. He follows me into the kitchen to get him a cheese stick, which he practically swallows in one gulp. I pat his sides. "That was weird, wasn't it, Chevy? What do you think about Uncle Richie?"

He barks.

"Yeah, me too."

He follows me into my room. I pull my sock drawer open and grab the lock from Cat's Cove. The metal is cold. I turn it over and examine the three scratches; they seem intentional.

I click on my desk lamp. My computer whirs as I review everything I know about The Cat, again. There must be something I've missed. It takes me twenty-two minutes and three seconds until I find it.

CHAPTER 26

Friday: 33 Minutes Until I Tell Patrick about the Clue

The next day at school, I can't decide if I should tell Patrick what I found out.

Brain says: He doesn't need to know anything. It's *our* treasure.

During lunch, we sit together, overlooking The Great Wave. I unwrap my turkey sandwich with no mayo and take a bite.

Patrick tosses a grocery bag onto the bench and begins unpacking. I count three frosted cupcakes, two small bags of Doritos, Sour Patch Kids, four Hawaiian rolls, a celery stick with peanut butter, two Yoo-hoos, three string cheeses, a bag of nuts that say *Omega-3*, and a tiny clementine.

He eyes my expression as he lays it all out. "What? I get hungry."

"Queen Bea packs you that?"

He smiles. "Some of it. I add the rest when she isn't looking." He unwraps a string cheese and shoves it into his mouth.

"So," he says, his mouth full of cheese. He flattens a notebook on his lap. "I've got everything all planned." His eyes shine. "The lunar eclipse happens this Monday—that's only in three days!"

I nod and swallow.

Brain says: I warned you not to get roped into this.

Patrick stands, too amped to sit. "After checking my charts, the optimum time for time travel that night is at 9:04 P.M."

I want to interrupt him, but I can't.

Brain says: Are we seriously doing this?

"That's when the sun, moon, and earth will line up and cover the full moon in complete darkness. Gravity will bend and create a wormhole, perfect for time travel." He shoves a cupcake in his mouth and brushes the crumbs from his face. He waits for my reaction.

Brain says: Tell him he's crazy.

Hush, Brain.

"Patrick, hold on."

"Yeah?" He runs one hand through his Einstein hair and shoves another cheese stick into his mouth.

"How do you know all of this exactly?" I throw the rest of my lunch away, not hungry anymore.

His eyes open wide as he swallows. "The internet, of course. Also, there are some really interesting time continuum books down at the library."

I nod.

"If you ever need help, ask the librarian, Mrs. Davenport, instead of the other one, Joe, because she's way more patient and open-minded."

I smile. Patrick's always trying to make everyone else's life a little easier. Kind of like how Minny was when she lived here. I feel bad about what I said in my text.

He continues, "I've made a list of all the supplies we'll need, including some headlamps, but—" He checks something on his list. "I've already ordered those."

Brain says: Tell him how unreliable you are.

My heart bumps.

Brain says: Girls who have panic attacks and can't even order food at IHOP can't be seconds. Girls who can't help their cousins can't be seconds.

I can't help anyone—not even myself.

I feel Brain nodding.

"Patrick," I say.

I expect him to talk over me, but he doesn't.

"Patrick, I . . ."

"Do you want a copy of my list? Because I can email it to you." His pen's poised, ready to write down my address.

Brain says: Tell him about the monster—the monster is you.

"What is it?" Patrick asks, his face earnest.

Finally, I say, "Are you sure you know how to build a time machine?"

He doesn't even blink. "It's online."

A breeze ripples over the sea of grass in front of Las Olas Middle School—dandelions and trees sway—leaves fall from their branches.

Brain says: Tell him.

I wrap my arms around myself.

I take a deep breath. "Why don't you ask Natasha from your STEAM class to be your second-in-command? She probably already knows everything about this stuff."

Brain says: Coward.

"Natasha? My second? No way. Plus, you'd be surprised at how opinionated she is." He smiles his toothy smile.

I ignore the heat that's crawling all over me.

"But I'm not the right person, I mean, under pressure, I'm not—" I search for the right word. "The best," I finish.

Brain says: A massive understatement.

Patrick seems surprised. "You're the perfect person. We need each other. I'll help you find The Cat's treasure. And you help me go back in time to see my parents. We're good-luck charms, I know it."

Brain says: Impossible.

Impossible, I know. But who does it hurt?

Brain says: Me. I have a horrible headache.

Me too. I feel like I've been walking around carrying dumbbells in my backpack since school began. It's only gotten worse since Minny left. Dr. Rosenthal says I need a friend. Why not Patrick?

Slowly, I nod. In less than eight seconds I've made up my mind. "All right," I say. "Let's do it."

"Yes!" says Patrick. "You won't be sorry."

The bell rings.

He slings his backpack over his shoulder.

"Wait, Patrick," I say. "I have to tell you something."

Brain holds his breath.

"You know the scratches we found on the lock with no keyhole?"

He nods. "So violent."

I squeeze my hands together. "The guy who runs the blog about The Cat lives right here in La Quinta Beach! He's a retired police officer who used to work on the case."

Patrick's face doesn't change.

"Don't you get it? If we can find that guy, then maybe he'll look at what we found and tell us if it's from The Cat."

"Nice," says Patrick, pumping his fist into the air. He holds up his hand for me to give him a high five.

Brain says: Don't.

I slap Patrick's waiting hand.

"Yes, another Cora-five! We're going to find that treasure!"

Brain says: You're going to regret it.

Hush, Brain.

I follow Patrick through the quad, feeling lighter than before.

Patrick says, "Long live seconds!"

CHAPTER 27

17 Minutes Until The Cat Is in Plain Sight

*M*ondays and Fridays I help Mom and Dad at their stores. Mondays are usually for Little Boy Blue and Fridays are for Custom Ride. I pedal my bike hard as I fly down the street to Custom Ride.

It feels good to have the possible treasure-clue in my possession and to be a part of Patrick's crazy time travel team. The bowling ball in my stomach has disappeared. I think I might like being a second.

Brain says: Stop it.

I stop at Piedmonts' Seaside Gifts because Dad loves an afternoon Fudgsicle.

I take out my phone and stare at the last thing Minny and I texted.

Minny: r u mad at me

Me: No. I don't know.

My heart bumps. I do know. I'm not mad at her. I'm mad at myself. I don't want her to be unhappy and to not have friends. If she were here now, she'd be happy for me that I've made friends with Patrick. Minny always wants the best for me.

I text Minny: I'm not mad.

Then I text: I'm at Piedmonts'.

Minny texts: Tell Mr. Piedmont I sd hi !!!!!!!!!! I'm gld we're nt in a fight I miss La Quinta And I miss u 2 ☺

I hesitate and then text her: ☺ ☺ ☺ ☺ ☺ <3 <3 <3 <3 <3 <3

Brain says: That's overboard on the emojis.

But that's how I feel.

The bell dings as I walk in.

Minny used to yell, "Hi, Mr. Piedmont, it's Paulo's girls." She said this even though technically she's not *Paulo's girl,* but Mr. Piedmont loves my dad and lets us do whatever we like. Dad always helps him with his cars for free.

Along with the Fairfield Park T-shirts and La Quinta Beach hats, Mr. Piedmont has an ice cream freezer in the back—one dollar per frozen treat, but he never makes me pay. He also sells swimsuits, sunscreen, shovels, shells, and postcards, anything a tourist would like.

I grab a Fudgsicle for Dad and a freeze-dried ice cream, Mini Dots, for me.

Mom says Mr. Piedmont put the freezer in for his grandkids, who come over on the weekends. When they're in town, she calls it the Piedmont Reign of Terror. In the summer, if we run out of change at The Little Boy Blue, I come here. I don't mind Mr. Piedmont's grandkids. They can be cute.

Brain says: I think the word you're looking for is *beastly*.

I weave through the clothes racks and seashell collections.

"Hello, there," says Mr. Piedmont. He's short and squat, like an old raisin. His hat says *Vitamin Sea*. He stands up from behind a shelf and brushes at his knees. "I was just doing a little inventory."

As I follow him to the cash register, I worry that maybe he'll forget that I'm Dad's daughter. Usually Minny does all the talking. My stomach churns.

He leans heavily against the counter as I place the ice cream there. My hand shakes. He taps my container of Birthday Cake Mini Dots. "Only one today? Where's your little friend?"

I wipe my hands on my shorts. "Moved." I gulp.

"Ah, so sad. But changes give you lots of new opportunities." He smiles.

I wait. Am I supposed to say something? My mind goes blank.

Finally, he says, "No charge."

Relief washes over me. I can breathe again.

"Tell your dad I've got my eye on that 1973 roadster he's refurbishing. Reminds me of my missus."

Mrs. Piedmont died a long time ago—he still has a framed photo of her behind the counter. She sits mid-laugh, in a wicker chair in front of a large parrot.

He hands me a paper bag with the ice cream just as something catches my eye. A yellowed newspaper article hangs on the wall, right next to Mrs. Piedmont's photo. The headline says *Local Woman Spies Billionaire Tech Recluse Catherine Van*

Larr. Mrs. Piedmont stands on the pier, her hair wind-whipped, squinting into the sun.

I freeze. *Cat's Cove. The crash.*

I can't believe I never noticed it before.

Mr. Piedmont knows something about that night?

My heart pounds.

"Mr. Piedmont," I stammer.

Already, he's moved on, busy counting lip balm. "Yes, ma'am. What can I do for you? Do you want to trade out those Mini Dots? I have it on good authority the Birthday Cake ones have lost their luster."

I shake my head and point at the wall behind him. "Is." My voice cracks. "Is that your wife?"

He spins around and plucks the parrot photo off the wall. "My Violet? Oh yes, she loved birds. Especially exotic ones." He coughs. "She could spend all day at Emerald Bird Sanctuary. Have you been?"

I shake my head. "The newspaper article," I whisper-say.

Brain says: If you're not going to speak up, why even bother?

"This?" He pulls it from the wall. The corners of his mouth turn up. "Violet's fifteen minutes of fame. She was very proud." He hands it to me. "Most people around here remember that night like it was yesterday." He balances the lip balm carefully in the display case. "You weren't even born then."

My overheated face starts to calm. "What happened?"

"Violet and I had just opened Piedmonts' Seaside Gifts— twenty-five years in business—thank you very much." He proudly raises his chin. "We'd been up late working on display windows for Halloween. The grunion were running that night, so there were a lot of people at the beach. I was hoping to finish a little early because Violet had just left to relieve our babysitter—when out of nowhere there's a gigantic BOOM, like Judgment Day." He claps his hands.

I jump.

His eyes widen. "Supersonic. I swear, the whole building shook. For a second I thought it was the Big One, but the boom didn't reoccur. Then a fleet of fire trucks flew down the street—sirens blazing. Immediately, I locked the store and headed down to the jetty."

"You went down there?" I breathe.

"They had pretty well taped everything off with caution tape when I got there, but I could still see flames burning on the water. A crowd had formed. People said it was a small plane."

"What about your wife?"

His voice turns hushed. "She got stuck at one of the road-blocks, and that's when *it* happened." He leans down, closer—his eyes dark, like the deepest blue of the ocean.

"What *it*?" I whisper-say.

"She thinks she saw her, Catherine Van Larr."

I suck in my breath. "They never found her body."

He nods. "At least, that's what Violet told the police." He slaps the counter. "They took a report and then later a guy from the local paper came and did this write-up."

I examine the photo more closely. I can't believe I never noticed this before. "How did she know it was her?"

"She said she was driving down an alley near La Vista, trying to get home around the police tape and flashing lights, when she saw someone limp across the road and disappear into the bushes. And even though she said it seemed off-kilter, she sped up. She thought they might need help."

I lean against the display case and all the ChapSticks fall.

Brain says: Good one.

"I'm sorry," I say, mortified. I start to kneel to pick them up.

"Leave it," he says, fully into his story. "As she got closer, she saw a woman hunched in the shadows. Violet rolled down her window to ask if she needed help when a car pulled up behind her. The headlights flashed. When she looked back, the woman was gone. Instead, a large cat sat smack in the middle of the road."

I shiver.

Brain says: A ghost cat.

Now Mr. Piedmont and I kneel, scooping the ChapSticks into a bowl.

"But why?" I ask. "Why would she want to disappear?"

He shrugs. "I don't know. But there are all sorts of people who want to be left alone in this world. Maybe she's one of them. I heard she's off in Argentina living on the beach, spending her billions."

"What do you think about her gold coins?"

He adjusts his hat. "I've looked for them myself. But I think if they were out there, they'd have washed up by now. Some-one would've found them."

My stomach knots. I help him put the ChapSticks away. "But she couldn't turn into a cat, could she?" I ask.

"You don't think so?" Then he winks, like he's teasing. "The world's full of all sorts of mysteries."

I shove the ice cream into my backpack and pause. Usually I slip out the door without saying a word, but today I look him in the eye. "Thank you."

"Thank you! And tell your mom and aunt to come say hey. I miss seeing those twins!"

I jump on my bike and head toward Custom Ride.

Brain says: You didn't believe all that, did you?

I don't know what to believe. I have to talk to Dad.

In two minutes and thirteen seconds I burst through Dad's office door. "You'll never guess what Mr. Piedmont said!" But then I stop. It's not Dad sitting at the desk.

It's Uncle Richie.

"Hi," he says. He doesn't get up.

I eye him suspiciously.

He clears his throat. "Your dad will be back in a second." He's wearing one of Dad's shirts again. It says *Custom Ride, Vintage Originals*.

I stand there, awkwardly clutching the paper bag to my chest.

Brain says: What's he doing out again?

Yeah, what's going on with that? Why is Uncle Richie around, always taking over Dad's life? My heart thumps.

"Are you out of rehab?" I stammer.

His face begins to redden. "No, I'm still in rehab. They only let me out with certain 'safe people' to give me a reprieve."

"Like a reward?"

He swallows hard. "Yes, something like that. Rehab can be pretty—dark. Hardest thing I've ever done." He's now as red as I've ever seen a person. As red as me.

The cold from the ice cream leaks through the paper and freezes my hand. "So, Dad's like your helper?"

He nods. "Yes."

We sit there and stare at one another.

1 2 3 4 5

I count the books on Dad's bookshelf.

Finally, he says, "What do you have there?"

The door opens. "Cor-Bell!" Dad says. He gives me a big bear hug. "You just missed someone—a friend, I think. He was looking for you." His eyebrows raise in a question.

I hand Dad his partially melted Fudgsicle and suddenly feel bad that I didn't bring one for Uncle Richie.

"Thank you, I was just thinking I needed one of these. You know, three o'clock slump," Dad says.

Uncle Richie laughs—that's when I see the resemblance. Their eyes crinkle in just the same way.

I hold my Mini Dots out to Uncle Richie.

He shakes his head no.

"Who was here?" I ask.

"Mom texted and said there was some kid at the house asking for you, so I told her to send him here, since it's Friday.

He waited for a while, but then said he had to go prepare for some kind of training."

"Space training," Uncle Richie interrupts.

Why'd I have to stay so long at Piedmonts'?

"What's he training for?" Dad asks.

Brain says: The idiot games.

Suddenly I feel protective of Patrick's time machine dream, no matter how impossible it sounds. "Uh. Cross-country," I say. I know what it's like to have people think you're out of your mind. "Dad, can I go? I've got to catch up with that kid," I say, heading out the door.

"Cor, you just got here. Uncle Richie and I want to hear about your treasure. We're thinking of going out to Cat's Cove tomorrow, if he gets a pass, to check it out—for old times' sake."

Brain says: Uncle Richie has replaced you.

My stomach feels tight, like a fist. Maybe he needs Dad more than me.

I wait.

Dad nods. "Fine. You can go."

"Sorry, Dad. I'll show it to you later." The door slams behind me.

CHAPTER 28

9 Minutes and 30 Seconds Until I Act Like Not-Cora

*F*riday night, Mom circles Fairfield Park parking lot, again, and I'm reminded that I really, really hate amusement parks. What am I doing here?

Brain says: This is the worst idea ever.

I do deep breathing because I've momentarily lost my mind.

Brain says: Not my fault.

Patrick texted me that he had time travel training tonight—something that can only be done at Fairfield Park. And normally, I won't go near this place, but Patrick—for a big sheepdog boy—has excellent skills of persuasion. "I need my second," he said.

Mom steps on the brake to avoid running over a family. "Let me just park the car," she says.

"I want to go to Fairfield Park," whines Sunshine from the back seat. "I never get to do anything fun."

Brain says: That's inaccurate.

Tonight, Fairfield Park is packed. Neon lights flash across the interior of our car as the roller coaster, the Sidewinder, screeches past. Exhaust piles around us as we sit in parking-lot traffic.

Minny texts: I wnt 2 go 2 fairfield don't 4get 2 get cotton candy

I text: I hate cotton candy.

My stomach churns.

Brain says: This is the worst decision you've ever made.

Mom tries Parking Lot C. "Don't worry, Cora. Somebody's bound to leave. I'll walk you inside and make sure you find Patrick."

I nod.

"And your cell phone has a full charge?" she asks.

I nod again.

Mom's hopeful with the prospect of me joining kids my age at Las Olas Middle School on a typical Friday night activity. I do deep breathing to calm my nerves.

We circle the parking lot again. The parking stalls are packed.

"Why can't I go to Fairfield Park with Cora?" whines Sunshine.

"Not tonight, sweetie." Mom honks at a BMW blocking traffic. "Of all days to come to Fairfield Park, the weekends really are the worst."

"Sorry," I say. "Patrick said—"

"I know. I know," says Mom. "An emergency."

Sunshine's atoms vibrate through the car. "If Dad were here, he'd let me go to Fairfield Park with Cora."

"You could've stayed home with him if you wanted to." Mom circles the parking lot again. "Blast this traffic." She grumbles into her Diet Coke.

"Sorry, Mom."

My cell phone dings.

Patrick texts: Where are you?!

I text: In the parking lot. Mom can't find a space.

Patrick texts: Just have her drop you off. I'm at the entrance!!!!!

Brain says: Don't do it. DON'T.

Hush, Brain. I have to think.

This is what Dr. Rosenthal and Mom and Minny always wanted me to do. Try new things. Get out of my comfort zone. I visualize myself standing next to Patrick.

"Mom," I say. "I think I'll be okay if you drop me off."

Mom takes a deep breath. "I don't know, Cora."

"Patrick's waiting just inside the entrance."

My phone dings again.

Patrick texts: I got you a cotton candy!!!

"Maybe something will open up," Mom says.

"Let's do affirmations!" Sunshine bounces behind us.

I shake my head.

"I have my cell phone if *anything* happens," I remind Mom.

Mom and I both know that's code word for panic attack.

179

She chews on the inside of her cheek—"Are you sure, Cora?" Slowly, she maneuvers the car over to Passenger Loading and Unloading. Kids, just like me, get in and out of waiting cars.

"Do you need an affirmation?" asks Sunshine.

I shake my head.

Brain says: You're in over your head.

"Okay." Mom hands me money. "This is why we've been practicing Social Skills. We want you to be able to do things on your own."

I nod.

Sunshine pokes her head out from behind my seat, her face perched between Mom and me, like a cherry on an ice cream sundae. "Affirmations!"

"No." My heart flutters.

Sunshine says, "Say, I am strong and smart and that's how everyone sees me." She smiles with all her teeth. Then she kisses my hand that's perched on the headrest between us.

I pretend to wipe it off. "Say it," say Mom and Sunshine together.

"Please," Mom says weakly. "It'll make me feel better for you." She gives my same hand a squeeze.

Together we say, "I am strong and smart and that's how everyone sees me." Our eyes meet. Our laughs bounce off each other, filling our car with happy photons.

Behind us, someone honks.

"I'm okay," I say, mostly for myself.

"And the minute you text me, I'll be right here, at this spot, to pick you up." Mom's eyes are wide.

"Got it." I open the door and step out onto the curb as the night closes around me. The sounds from the amusement park stab my ears. And before I can really think about what I'm doing, Mom and Sunshine pull away.

Sunshine hangs out of the window. "Good luck with Social Skills! Bring me back a Fairfield Park giant gobstopper—I've wanted one my whole life!"

I pull up my hoodie to protect myself from the neon and the screams and the blippy music.

I'm alone, in a place I hate.

Brain says: You dragged us here. Now you can get us out.

CHAPTER 29

22 Minutes and 45 Seconds Until I'm Shaked and Baked

*H*ow did I forget that at the beginning of sixth grade, Minny said at least half of Las Olas Middle School hangs out at Fairfield Park on the weekends? I squint at the neon. Why didn't I bring sunglasses or earmuffs or earplugs?

I get into line behind two ladies and do deep breathing.

Ando and his group are in line ahead of me. They haven't noticed me; they're too busy throwing sunflower seeds into people's hair. They throw one at a middle-aged woman and it sticks nicely in her bun without her noticing. They cheer.

The lady ahead of me turns around. "Can I help you?"

I shake my head. Am I standing too close?

Brain says: Acting normal is exhausting.

I pay the entrance fee, fifteen dollars, and walk through the Fairfield Park archway covered with paintings of neon dolphins with bulging eyes and too happy smiles.

Brain says: Dolphins have a permanent curvature of the mouth. They're forced to smile.

The concrete walkway's covered in scuff marks and chewed gum. I wait by the amusement park map.

I text Patrick: `Where are you?`

Then add: `! ! ! ! ! ! ! !`

He texts: `Octopus Spin!! Meet me here!!`

I text: `WHY AREN'T YOU AT THE ENTRANCE?`

He texts: `sorry`

My heart thunders.

Brain says: Worst idea ever.

The park map blurs. I do deep breathing and stand behind a trash can as Ando and his group pass.

It takes me four minutes and twenty-three minutes to find the Octopus Spin.

Brain says: I'm an excellent map reader. You're not welcome.

The Octopus Spin is tucked in between the Whack-a-Jellyfish and the bathrooms. It's a massive purple octopus at least twenty feet high with arms that swing children gently around and around. Some kids smile. But to me it's—

Brain says: It's terrifying.

Exactly.

Sunshine would love it.

I wait. And wait. And wait. The lights glow brighter. The screaming gets louder. Still I wait. The back of my neck itches.

I text Patrick. `Where r u?`

He doesn't respond.

My stomach clenches. Why did I ever agree to meet Patrick?

I scan the people near the Whack-a-Jellyfish, no Patrick. I

scan the people waiting at the bathrooms. No Patrick. Could there be another purple octopus somewhere else in the park?

The lights from the Ferris wheel reflect on puddles. Kids shriek as the octopus arms swing them around, their faces like ghosts. Someone splashes through the puddle water. Drops sprinkle across my shoes.

Breathe, Cora.

Brain says: You should've listened to me.

I know.

Brain says: Patrick's a forced friend. He's not real.

I know.

It takes less than eight minutes to make a bad decision. I turn back the way I came. A crowd of people envelops me. Nothing but bodies, and faces, and talking. I squeeze my eyes shut and wrap my arms around myself. How will I ever get out of here?

"Helloooo!"

I open my eyes.

Patrick stands in front of me, waving a cotton candy. Patrick, with his stupid sheepdog face and his stupid alien backpack. "Here."

Brain says: Cotton candy fixes nothing!

I wave the cotton candy away.

"Where are you going?" he asks, putting his hand lightly on my shoulder.

I jerk away, my heartbeat thumping against the backs of my eyes.

"You're still coming to time travel training, aren't you? I'm sorry I wasn't here. I had some important questions for Larry, the guy who fixes the hydraulics on the Octopus Spin."

The crowd passes us. Now it's just Patrick and me standing under the spinning lights. His eyes are shadowed.

"I've been waiting for eight minutes and five seconds. You should have met me at the entrance." My voice shakes. "I don't go to Fairfield Park *ever*."

Patrick stops smiling. "I'm sorry. I thought you'd be okay meeting me here." He pauses. "Do you want to go home?"

Lights flash. People scream as a roller coaster flies by. A siren blares from the Whack-a-Jellyfish game.

"I don't think I can," I say.

His mouth scrunches up. "You're the only one I trust with time travel notations."

Brain says: No! We are out of here. O-U-T.

I visualize walking back through the belly of Fairfield Park—the lights, the noise, the people. It's so exhausting. And Mom would be disappointed that I couldn't even last half an hour.

"Please say you'll stay. I promise I won't leave your side again."

"Fine," I say. "I'll stay."

Brain says: Why won't you listen to me? How can I protect you if you won't listen??

I ignore him.

Brain says: My only job is to keep you safe.

I shake my head. *Shut up, Brain.*

Patrick gives me a high five. "Yes! You're staying!"

I straighten my shoulders. I can do this. I can do all of it.

"Follow me. The Shake and Bake's this way," says Patrick. So, I do.

I step in a puddle—my high-top gets soaked. Patrick walks ahead of me, fast.

"Wait, I thought your training was on the Octopus Spin," I say, pointing to the little-kid ride.

Patrick makes a face at its sluggish rotation. Parents wave at their preschoolers. "This baby ride? No way. Come on!" The bag of cotton candy swings at his side.

I try to keep up with him, but his pace is just too jubilant. It's like walking with Sunshine, *zip zip zip*, except worse—because Patrick's legs are longer.

"It's just around the corner," Patrick says over his shoulder. His hair looks even bigger than normal, like it sucked up all the amusement-park energy. He waves at the guy working the game Rubber Your Ducky.

We stop at a food booth. "Hellloooo," Patrick says to the lady selling deep-fried things like Oreos, Twinkies, and sticks of butter. "We'll take two.

"My treat," he says to me. "Just what a time traveler and treasure hunter need for sustenance." He hands me a deep-fried Oreo on a stick, shiny with grease. We sit at a little table.

Patrick props up his feet.

Deep-fried Oreos taste like a newly found treasure. "How do you know all the people who work here?" I ask as I take another bite.

"They all play bingo with Queen Bea." His phone beeps—he

checks it. "Come on," he says, wiping his hands on his pants. "We've got a reserved place in line."

I follow him, hanging on to the sleeve of his sweatshirt. Turn left at the carousel and then straight ahead, until an awful sight looms before me. This can't be the Shake and Bake. A wobbly Ferris wheel lined with gaudy lights—a monstrosity of a ride—stands forty feet in the air. Perched at the end of each rickety arm is a self-contained basket that spins to the tempo of frantic music.

I feel sick.

Brain says: You should.

"Look at this beauty!" Patrick says, like it's the Orion Nebula. "Time travel training at its finest."

The giant crank in the middle spins faster and faster. Screams swoosh by, ear-piercing and then not, depending on how far away they are.

A worker, Amar—according to the name on his tag—walks up to us. His dark ponytail is like a waterfall down to his waist. "Pat, my main man," he says, giving Patrick a high five. "You back for more?"

Patrick nods exuberantly.

"Space travel training, coming right up!" Then Amar notices me. "I see you've brought a lady friend. Space travel training for two?"

On cue, my face is ablaze.

He nods. "This is my friend Cora. And she's a girl . . ." Patrick's voice trails off.

The guy laughs as if Patrick's a comedian. "Okay, Casanova."

My body burns from head to toe. "I'm—I'm not going on that thing," I stammer. I pull my hoodie up for protection. It deflects the stares of the people waiting in line.

Pow. Pow. Pow.

The Shake and Bake pulses and creaks. Its appendages lumber around and around as people inside the cages shriek.

Panic starts in my toes.

Brain says: I told you not to come.

The line for the Shake and Bake wraps around the corner and through aisles created with iron stakes and rope. I wonder how long people have waited in line to ride something that will certainly kill them.

Amar slams the cage shut on a family of four—it looks like a mom, dad, brother, and little sister. The boy looks terrified as he grabs his mom's hand.

Patrick turns to me, his eyes bright. "You're going to love it."

I swallow. Vomit sits at the back of my throat. "I can't go."

Amar turns to us. "I can squeeze you into the front. Just remember, you've got to have my back at bingo, like usual." He winks. Apparently, this isn't the first time he's let Patrick skip to the front of the line. "Just tell Queen Bea to spin me some winning numbers!"

"We can't cut in front of all these people." Their glares bounce off my hoodie.

Patrick ignores me and nods at Amar. "That'd be awesome. Thanks!"

"No," I whisper-say.

Amar escorts us to the front of the line, right in front of

Ando and his group. I pull my hoodie tight around my face and hope no one recognizes me.

"We'll get you on the next one, kids," Amar says to them. "We've got two VIPs at Fairfield Park. It'll only be an extra eight minutes of your time." He has a dazzling smile.

Humberto, one of Ando's friends, says, "No way, man."

Angelica grumbles.

Someone puts their hand on my arm.

I turn.

"Cora," says Ando. "You're cutting in line?" His eyebrows arch—his mouth turns into a thin line.

"No, I—sorry," I say.

Patrick turns. "Hellllloooo!" He gives Ando a high five. "Sorry about making you wait. But we've got some important research going on."

"Yeah, right," says Humberto. "*Research*." He makes a kissing noise.

Patrick's unfazed as I turn even redder than I already am. I adjust my hoodie so they can't see my face.

"You ready?" Amar asks.

Brain says: Never. Don't do it.

Amar unlocks the last basket. He holds the door open—a bright red cage sits before us. "This one's the deluxe package." He flicks the alien bobblehead doll inside so it sways and jiggles, the rings spinning around its tiny axis.

"No," I say, as I clutch the handlebar attached to the outside.

"Come on, Cora," Patrick says, holding out a stopwatch

and a tiny notebook. His eyes plead. "Time travel research. You have to record the rotations. I need your big brain." He grabs my hand.

"Come on!" yells Humberto.

I gulp back the watery saliva that's pooled at the back of my throat and take the notebook. Even though I don't like to be touched, Patrick's hand feels nice.

"Let's go, lovebirds." Amar pushes us closer to the giant red mouth of the Shake and Bake.

"We're not lovebirds," Patrick says. "We're a research team."

"Whatever," says Amar.

Humberto continues the kissing noises.

My feet feel cemented to the ground.

"Come *on*," someone complains from the line.

My heart thunders.

Patrick gently pulls my hand. "You'll love it," he says. His fingers warm around mine, I let him lead me inside the cage.

"I—I—I can't do it." I squeeze my eyes shut.

"Don't close your eyes," Patrick says. "Where's your timer and the notebook?"

I fumble with them.

Brain says: Patrick picked the wrong second.

"When we get to the top, press the button, while—"

I sit, frozen.

"Here, put your seat belt on." He hands me the clasps.

They slip, but I finally get them locked.

Amar checks our seat belts and locks the cage from the

outside. Panic squeezes my chest. I'm trapped, and what's worse is the ride hasn't even begun.

Patrick points at the stopwatch again. "Now press this button when we get to the top, and I'm going to start mine when we're at the bottom—"

I take great gulping breaths and ignore my pounding head. Minny would never make me do this. Minny never made me do anything I didn't want to.

Curse Patrick.

"Get some, Patrick!" yells Humberto.

Curse Ando and his group.

The cage shudders and we begin to spin. Slow at first, then faster, faster—the alien bobblehead spins manically.

"Here we go!" yells Patrick over the noise.

I cling to the cage—the metal grate digs into my fingers. My body rocks back and forth, our cage tossed higher and higher.

Brain says: This is insanity.

"It's at rotation three that you'll really notice how the velocity starts to pick up, like real time travel. I'm recording the amount of time it takes to feel the turbulence, so this is where I need your timer to—" He stops. "Are you okay?"

I scrunch my eyes closed and try to ignore the nausea at the bottom of my stomach, getting stronger with each rotation. Gravity presses me flat against my seat as liquid at the back of my throat bubbles forward.

"Patrick," I say.

I clamp my hand over my mouth, trying to prevent disaster.

"Hold my hand," he says, reaching for it.

If only that would help.

Our cage spins faster. My stomach lurches. And no matter how I try not to, I vomit deep-fried Oreo all over the Shake and Bake's red, deluxe-model cage.

"Stop! Stop the training!" Patrick yells to Amar.

But the Shake and Bake labors around and around.

Throw up splatters us both. My stomach spasms.

Slowly the ride limps to a stop. My head spins as I dry heave.

I open my eyes. Patrick's T-shirt is covered in liquefied Oreo. The cage is splashed. My hair drips in foul-smelling bio-hazard.

I hiccup as I wipe my mouth with my T-shirt. Tears fill my eyes as I reach for the back of my head. It aches. I must have hit it on the cage during the ride.

"Whew!" Patrick says. He wipes his forehead with the back of his hand. His nose wrinkles in disgust.

Ugh.

Tears slide down my face and I don't even try to stop them. I cry for the vomit, and the embarrassment, and for making Ando and his group wait. I cry for making Patrick smelly and gross. I cry because I'm a horrible second and now Patrick, my only friend in La Quinta Beach, will never want me because I've thrown up all over him during time travel training and in front of practically the whole sixth grade.

Why did I think I could be anything different than what I am?

Brain says: You can't.

Patrick wipes his hands on his shirt. He won't look at me.

Amar opens the cage.

Ando and his friends stare, and the people behind them stare too. Their eyeballs shatter me.

I wipe my face, snotting all over myself.

Humberto says, "Gross!!! What a freak."

Ando's group laughs. Someone makes gagging noises.

"Code Hurricane George at the Shake and Bake, cage number one," Amar says into a walkie-talkie. He closes the line with a chain and a sign attached to it.

CAUTION: CLEANUP IN PROGRESS

"The Shake and Bake is closed, folks, for an indefinite amount of time." He motions to the people waiting in line. "You can wait or go find something else to ride." The crowd groans as Patrick leads me to the bathrooms.

Angelica's eyes narrow as she watches me. "Why do some people have to ruin everything?"

Patrick calls my mom from my phone. He waits with me at the entrance and continues to hand me a Mount Everest amount of napkins to try and clean up. I think he tries to talk to me, but I can't focus on what he's saying. I only know that I'm a vomitous, human tomato—burning up the atmosphere— burning up everyone around me.

Why would anyone ever want to be my friend?

Brain says: They don't.

CHAPTER 30

25 Minutes Until Mom Reveals Altman Family Secrets

*A*t home, I lie in the bath, with bits of Oreo floating in the water. Mom hasn't bothered me once. She said I can lie here as long as I want. So I do, even though the water's gone cold.

Sunshine knocks on the door. It's past her bedtime. "Cora, are you coming out? Mom saved orange chicken for you in the microwave."

My stomach clenches.

1 2 3 4 5 6

I count the lines in my pruned fingers.

"Cora?"

Mom shoos her away. So, this is what it's like to be shaked and baked. If I could muster more tears, I would, but they don't come. Patrick will never talk to me again. How could he after the vomit and humiliation? Obviously, I can't be trusted.

But it did feel nice, for a moment, to have a friend again. To be someone's second.

Quiet drips down the bathroom walls and fills my tub with everything sad.

I expect Dad to knock on the bathroom door, but he never does. Surely Mom has told him what happened. Parents think we don't know that they share information about their kids, but we know. They share everything, especially the bad news.

Mom has probably already made an appointment with Dr. Rosenthal. It's not hard to figure out what the doctor will say. *Visualize success. Do affirmations. Breathe. Count. Ignore Brain.*

Nothing works.

I don't think I like Dr. Rosenthal.

Brain says: Like her or not, no one can ever help you.

I get out of the water, goose bumps cover my body, and I realize there are no clean bath towels under the sink. I dry myself off with a hand towel, the one from Grandma Altman with the special embroidery, the one Mom only likes us to use for company. My toes are so shriveled with water they hurt when I walk.

Chevy whines at the door and bolts in when I open it. I poke my head out into the hallway. Sunshine's left an affirmation in front of the door.

It says *I am safe. My world is okay.*

I crumple it up and throw it in the garbage. I can't handle Sunshine, with her bounce, and her smile, and her brightness.

Brain says: She's the worst.

The floorboards creak as I creep down the hallway. I slip

into my bedroom and put on my favorite sweatshirt, the one that says *La Quinta Harbor*. Dad got it for me last year when we went to see another wrecked ship get added to the seawall. It was Labor Day. Normally, I'm not one for holidays because of all the people, but surprisingly the crowds weren't bad. Dad and I each got a corn dog and climbed onto the jetty to get a better view.

I text Minny: I have no friends.

I wait.

She doesn't respond.

Brain says: Forced friend.

Mom opens my bedroom door. "Are you all right?" she asks, her voice soft. "Your clothes are in the wash, so they'll be as good as new tomorrow."

I nod.

"I saved a plate of chicken for you. Are you hungry?"

All I can taste is vomit Oreos.

"Do you want to talk about it?"

"No. And I'm not hungry." My voice is barely a whisper.

She pats my hand. "I'll bring you a glass of water, okay?" Her forehead crinkles into a thousand wrinkles. She tucks a piece of hair behind her ear. "Your friend Patrick called."

My stomach makes a squelching sound.

"Cora, I know things didn't go well tonight, but I'm so proud of you for trying." She combs her fingers through my hair. "You were very brave."

I don't have the heart to tell her that my new friend is no longer mine. "Mom, stop," I say. I ruin everything.

"How's your head?" Mom asks, sitting on my bed.

"Fine. It's just a bump."

She sighs as if she's thinking of something sad. "We need to talk." She fiddles with her wedding ring. "You need to know why I'm mad at Dad and why I'm not a big fan of Uncle Richie."

I sit up straighter.

"I should have told you a while ago." She feels the back of my head with her fingers and presses gently. "Can you feel this?"

"What?"

"This scar. Here."

I walk my fingers to the place on my head and find a line of knotted flesh. Why have I never noticed it before?

Mom adjusts my comforter. "You've had it since you were one year old."

I hold my breath. "What happened?"

Mom hesitates. Her foot jiggles a million miles a second, like when we sit and wait in Dr. Rosenthal's office. Finally, she says, "Eleven years ago, Uncle Richie appeared from out of nowhere and wanted to work for Dad at Custom Ride. He said he was clean and sober, that he just needed a little help. I wasn't sure what to think. But Dad said that he could live here with us, because that's when Vo was so sick with cancer the first time."

I nod. "What does my head have to do with Uncle Richie?"

Mom puts a finger to my lips. "Just listen. Richie had been with us for about five or six months. He was fun and nice and

197

seemed to be doing well. Custom Ride had just been named Best New Business in La Quinta Beach. They had a ceremony and a fancy dinner." She shakes her head, remembering. "Dad and I were supposed to go, but I didn't want to leave you. Aunt Janet was out of town and Grandma Bell wanted to come with us to the ceremony. Eventually, I decided to stay home, but Dad wouldn't hear of it. He said Uncle Richie could watch you." She smiles. "Actually, Richie was really good with you, and I had only known him sober, so I figured it would be okay, for one night." She stops. Her smile fades.

My stomach begins to churn. I don't like this story.

She takes my hand. I don't pull it away.

"So, we left. You were ready for bed, snuggly in your jammies. All Richie had to do was give you a bottle and put you down for the night. At the dinner I couldn't get you out of my mind. Dad said I was a worrywart, but I only stayed long enough for him to receive his award. Then I left. I asked Grandma Bell to give Dad a ride home."

My heart thumps in my chest.

Mom's voice catches. "When I got back, I called for Richie, but there was no answer. I rushed to your room and flipped on the light. But you weren't in your crib. Instead, you were on the floor with blood on the back of your head. I called an ambulance."

"What happened to me?" I whisper-say, feeling the line of damaged flesh in my scalp.

"You fell out of your crib and it caused a subdural

hematoma; a small brain bleed. The doctors operated on you that night to relieve the pressure."

I suck in my breath. All these years, I thought my talking Brain was because of birth asphyxia, because I didn't breathe for eight minutes when I was born, but now—tears sting my eyes.

I have a talking Brain because of Uncle Richie?

Brain says: I knew he was bad.

Mom folds and refolds the baby blanket I still sleep with. "The doctors did an amazing job. They said they caught it just in time. You were fine. As good as new."

My heart thunders. I can't stop running my fingers along the scar.

"They gave you five stitches."

I feel where they were.

She reaches for my head—her fingers cover mine. "We think you tried to climb out of your crib and fell, hitting the corner of the dresser on the way down. The wood floors didn't do you any favors. You'd never climbed out of your crib before, so there was no way we could've known you could do it."

"Why didn't you tell me?"

She sighs. "You were so little. After doing brain scans, the doctors assured us you were completely fine. We just wanted to forget about it."

I pull my fingers away from my scar. "Where was Uncle Richie?"

"When he should've been babysitting you?" Mom's face

goes dark. "He was busy emptying the cash register at Custom Ride and stealing Dad's refurbished Land Cruiser."

Uncle Richie stole from Dad?

"Dad could never bring himself to press charges. We haven't seen him again since that night—until now."

Mom tugs me into a hug, and I let her.

Brain says: No amount of hugging can fix this.

"I'm sorry we kept that from you," she says. "Aunt Janet's been wanting me to tell you for a while now. She said you needed all the information so you could understand why Dad and I have been fighting. I know the tension hasn't been easy on you. And maybe it's been making your anxiety worse. Secrets aren't good for families." Mom pulls me away so she can read the expression on my face.

"Are you glad I told you?" Her eyes look hopeful. I can't make her feel like she made the wrong decision.

"Yes," I say, but my mouth tastes sour. Blood courses through my veins. Uncle Richie's the reason I fell? He's the reason I have a talking Brain? How could Dad ever let him in our house again?

CHAPTER 31

Saturday: 1 Hour and 3 Minutes Until I Realize Something about Friendship

I check my phone again. Minny still hasn't texted me back this morning. Figures. I take a deep breath and text her again. I have to know.

I text: `Were you my forced friend?`

She doesn't respond.

Mom lets me stay in bed, even though it's past ten.

My head hurts.

My heart hurts.

Betrayal sits in my stomach like a curdled milkshake from Fairfield Park. I don't know who I'm mad at. Mom? Dad? Uncle Richie? Minny? Maybe all four.

Chevy curls up with me in my comforter so I won't be lonely.

Sunshine has placed every stuffed animal she owns in a little parade across my bed. I heard Dad's car leave this morning, probably going to rehab.

I reach for my always-there-but-now-I-know-it scar. It's a

little sore from where I hit my head on the Shake and Bake. Uncle Richie really left me by myself? Uncle Richie stole money and a car from Custom Ride?

I feel like I swallowed the entire La Quinta Bay.

My door swings open. Sunshine bounces in and pats her stuffed penguin, who sits on the edge of my bed. "Is Chilly helping you feel better?"

I nod.

She gives me a handmade card. It says in Mom's handwriting, "There's nowhere to go but up," along with a picture of a Ferris wheel and two people and some balloons. "That's me and you," she says, pointing to the people. She grabs the penguin and tucks him underneath her chin.

"Where are you getting these affirmations?"

She taps her forehead. "From my brain, duh."

Of course.

"And Mom."

She nods and picks up a purple pig and dances it across my dresser. "Mom wants to know if you're feeling better, but I'm not supposed to bother you. Am I bothering you?" She makes a mustache on her stuffed animal with the end of her long ponytail.

"You should make me another card."

She throws the pig on the floor. "Okay!" She runs out my door, but then pokes her head back in. "I forgot. Someone's here for you."

Ugh.

"It's a boy." She giggles like a maniac.

Double ugh.

How could Patrick even want to see me? The spinning, the vomit, the embarrassment. He needs a different second; someone with a proper brain.

"Tell him I'm asleep."

"But you're not asleep."

"Sunshine!"

Her eyes widen.

"Fine, tell him I'm sick and I can't come out because I don't want him to catch it." She saw the vomit last night.

"Okeydokey, artichokey." She closes the door behind her.

Chevy looks out the window and growls.

"That's right, Chevy. Protect me."

I lift my curtain and wait to see Patrick's bouncy walk and electric hair. He's probably come over to tell me that he can no longer rely on a weirdo-vomit-tomato.

But it's not Patrick. I rub my eyes.

It's Ando. His skateboard glints in the sun as he walks across our lawn. He pauses for a second, then turns around to look at my house. I duck behind the window. How does he even know where I live?

My heart might jump out of my throat. Why is Bernando Mendez at my house and without his group of friends? What could he possibly want? Even alone, I feel myself turning red. Everyone from Las Olas Middle School saw what happened last night.

Finally, I get up and get dressed because I can't stand lying in bed any longer.

"Is Dad home yet?" I ask Sunshine as I walk into the kitchen.

"Dad went to a family therapy session with Uncle Richie. Mom wouldn't let me go," she says, sitting at the kitchen island.

"Of course Mom wouldn't let you go. You can't go to therapy with Dad and Uncle Richie."

"But Mom and Dad go to therapy with you." She snaps a Lego into place, but then wrecks her creation.

"They only sit in the waiting room," I respond.

Sunshine doesn't say anything.

"Do you want me to make you a quesadilla?" I ask.

"Yes!"

"Okeydokey, artichokey." I feel bad for Sunshine. She can't help it that she's only five and doesn't understand the family drama that exists right now with Aunt Janet and Uncle Richie. I barely understand it.

I pull out the ingredients—tortillas, cheese, butter—and place them on the counter. "Salsa?" I hold up the jar.

She makes a face.

I get out a large pan and turn on the burner. This is the only way to make a real quesadilla. They're not even good when they're microwaved. I spread the butter on both sides of the tortilla, add shredded cheese, top it with another tortilla, and place it in the pan. Voilà. The butter sizzles.

"What's all this?" Mom asks, coming in from the garage.

Sunshine smiles. "Cora's making me a snack because I'm *bored*."

Mom laughs. "What a great big sister you have." She looks at me. "Are you okay?"

I nod, considering my insides feel more shaked and baked than my outsides.

I hand Sunshine her quesadilla on a plate.

Mom raises her eyebrows. "I just got off the phone with Aunt Janet. I told her about last night."

"Mom!" Does the whole world need to know that I vomited on the Shake and Bake?

"Not about Fairfield Park. I told her about *our talk*."

"Is she still mad at me? About what happened with Blue?" I can hardly bear to hear the answer.

Mom smiles. It's her real one—nothing plastic about it. "Cora, honey, Aunt Janet wasn't mad at you. She was mad at me."

"But Blue broke his arm when I was babysitting."

"That could've happened with anyone. She's mad at *me* for not being honest with you. I should have told you sooner." She gives me a sheepish look. "I'm glad I finally listened to my sister."

"Me too." I give her a hug.

Brain says: What's with all this hugging?

"And guess what?" Mom asks. "We're going over to the Little Boy Blue. We've got to help Aunt Janet with the sidewalk sale."

"Finally!" Sunshine says. She pumps her arm into the air, just like Patrick. Poor Patrick, last night sitting in shock with my chocolate vomit in his hair.

Mom hands me my phone. "Why don't you give Patrick a call? He came by this morning while you were still asleep."

"That wasn't Patrick, that was—someone else." My face feels flushed, but if Mom notices, she doesn't say anything.

"No, it was Patrick," Mom says. "Bouncy kid with the big hair? I'm pretty sure I remember him."

I stare at Sunshine.

"He was the first boy who asked if you were feeling better, but I told him to go away." Melted cheese drips from her mouth.

"Sunshine!" I say.

"Mom said you were sick, so I told him to go home."

Mom steals a quesadilla triangle from Sunshine's plate and takes a large bite. "Patrick said something about bingo and research. That he needed his second? Does any of that make sense to you?"

My heart bumps. He still wants to be my friend? Even if he's a forced friend?

"Text him. You have to hang on to a friend like that." Mom smiles.

When I pick up my phone, I see that he's already texted me.

Patrick texts: I'm not mad because you threw up.

I text:

Patrick texts: Why would I be mad at you?

I text:

Patrick texts: It's your stomach's fault.

I text:

Patrick texts: And my fault for making you get on the Shake and Bake.

I text:

Patrick texts: Ride with me to seaside beach resort. I need my second.

I text: Okay.

Mom puts my bike in the back of her car. Aunt Janet says she has a sidewalk sale emergency. Not an emergency *emergency*, but a Little Boy Blue emergency. I hope it has everything to do with making new tags. My specialty.

"Come on, Sunshine," yells Mom from the driveway.

Sunshine bounds into the car, carrying a gigantic beach bag.

"What's that?" I ask.

"Stuff I need." The bag falls open—stuffed animals, Dad's fishing hat, bracelets, markers—is that a box of cereal? "I don't know how long we're going to be there."

Mom gets in and spies the bag. "I said you can't bring all of that stuff. Pick two things."

"I can't pick two," whines Sunshine.

Thank goodness I'm not stuck at the Little Boy Blue with Sunshine all day. Patrick's coming to the shop so we can ride to some beach club together. I have the treasure / lock in my pocket, just like he asked me to bring.

"Fine, whatever." Mom slams the car door and pulls out of our driveway.

I text Patrick: I hate Fairfield Park.

Patrick texts: You should have told me

I text: Ok. I hate Fairfield Park.

Patrick texts: I know. You threw up all over it. ☺ ☺ ☺

CHAPTER 32

37 Minutes Until I Learn More about Vomit Friends

The white twinkle lights on the Little Boy Blue canopy sparkle. I crawl through the blue miniature-sized door the shop has for little kids next to the regular door right beside it.

"Little boy blue, come blow your horn," I call through the door.

Aunt Janet's at the counter, wrapping something. "The sheep's in the meadow, the cow's in the corn," she responds in her usual way, finishing the nursery rhyme. The customer she's helping smiles.

People wander the store, looking through racks of clothes. It's busier than I thought it would be. Sunshine runs to the back to find Blue.

Mom stops at the tables out front to talk to Natalie, the college girl who works here. Mom organizes the hair things and jewelry on the tables, then she comes in. "I'm here. I'm here. I've got the extra sale signs."

Aunt Janet is frazzled. "You're saving my bacon. It's way busier than I thought it would be." She spies me in the corner, behind a stack of footed pajamas. "Cora, just finish up this last bow, while I run and show your mom where I need her help."

I gulp.

The lady at the checkout turns in my direction. She doesn't look bugged.

"Okay." I take Aunt Janet's place behind the counter. Spools of ribbons, the colors of the rainbow, stretch out in front of me.

"You're a lifesaver." Aunt Janet follows Mom to the stockroom.

The woman at the cash register eyes me, like maybe she thinks I don't know what I'm doing.

"What color would you like?" I ask, reminding myself to speak up. I try to keep myself from turning red.

"Whatever you think would look nice." Her glasses reflect the twinkle lights from the window. My heart bumps. I pull a navy-blue ribbon from the roll. "I think this looks nice."

"Love it." She checks her watch.

I tie the ribbon and place the Little Boy Blue sticker in the corner, just so. I hand the gift box to her. "Is this okay?"

"Perfect." She smiles at me. "I love seeing young people working hard and using their brains instead of glued to some screen. I commend you, young lady." She takes her box and marches out the door.

I smile. Yes, good job to me.

Aunt Janet comes back. "Oh, did she leave already? Was it all okay?" She looks a little worried.

"It was totally fine. She said I did a good job and that she likes to see kids my age using our brains."

Brain says: Brains are best when they're used.

Aunt Janet laughs. "That's Mrs. Rodenpike. She comes in every month and buys a dress for her granddaughter. She's not always easy to please, but I'd say she knows a good egg when she sees one."

An hour later, Patrick rides his bike to the Little Boy Blue. He says bingo is held at the Seaside Beach Resort and I have to come. I haven't ever been to the Seaside Beach Resort and I probably hate bingo. Mostly, I want to go home and get back into bed, but Patrick insists there's someone I have to meet today. It's a surprise.

Mom pulls my bike out of the back of her car. "Get back in the saddle," she says into my ear. "It's a new day."

Patrick shakes Mom's and Aunt Janet's hands before we leave. The sisters give each other an amused look. And then, I am free.

We ride down Mission, the air cool. The sun bright.

"You have the treasure we found, right?" Patrick asks.

"Yeah, how is this going to help again?" I still can hardly look at him, since all I remember is him covered in my vomit. I feel myself redden at the thought.

"You'll see!" He glides by me with his hand up—waiting for a high five.

I slap it.

"Yes! A Cora-five!" Patrick does a weird bicycle-victory dance that involves crashing into a streetlight.

"I'm okay!" he says.

I laugh, even though Brain doesn't like it.

Brain says: Why do you like *him*?

We ride across the parking lot of a low white building and get off our bikes.

"You're going to thank me later," Patrick says. He locks our bikes around a RESERVED FOR VETS sign and then holds the door open for me. "It's just through here."

The Seaside Beach Resort isn't really a beach resort. It's a retirement center. Also, it doesn't overlook the beach. It overlooks a Bob's Big Boy and a muffler repair.

"We're just in time for the early bird game," Patrick checks his phone. Voices come from down the hall. "Come on. You're going to *love* it. Are you sure you've never been to bingo before?"

I shake my head. "How is bingo going to help us find The Cat's gold?"

"Patience. Plus, you're going to have the best time of your life." Patrick bounces ahead. The last time he said that we were getting on the Shake and Bake.

My stomach churns.

"Helloooo, Mrs. Gitney. Sorry I'm late." Patrick does

this weird little shuffle-step dance while he talks. Two old women sit at a table and eye me, one the color of cooked fish.

A large sign reads SUNDAY BINGO LIVE. $100 CASH PRIZE. $25 PER PERSON FOR DESSERT, 4 CARDS, AND 2 DRINKS. 3:15 DOORS OPEN. 4:00 BINGO BEGINS.

It's 3:56 P.M.

The lady with long gray hair and the fish-face holds a cash box close to her chest. The other, dressed in head to toe white, Mrs. Gitney, examines a clipboard.

"Queen Bea's been asking for you," says Mrs. Gitney.

"Sorry, I had to get my friend."

"And who's this?" she asks.

I feel myself turn red.

"This is my friend Cora," says Patrick. "She's not here to play. Her presence is purely educational."

The fishy lady eyes me skeptically. "Fine." I feel her dismay at not getting her twenty-five dollars.

"Hurry along." Mrs. Gitney precisely crosses something off her list. "It's going to start any minute."

"Come on."

I follow Patrick through the door.

"Hellloo!" His voice bounces against the walls. The room's filled with folding tables and chairs. A long desk with coffee, cookies, and brownies is set against the wall. Mostly old people sit with bingo cards in front of them. There are a few tables of younger people sprinkled throughout, but no one here is as young as Patrick or me. People turn. A murmur flows through the room.

"Patrick!"

"You can start now. Patrick's here."

"Good to see you, Pat, my boy." An old guy in a blue jump-suit pats Patrick on the back. "I've got your seat all ready, right next to me."

"Thanks, Mr. Hernandez. But I'm on duty tonight—helping Queen Bea with the cards."

Patrick grabs my arm and pushes us past the tables. "Queen Bea can't stand it when I'm late." It's not easy to hurry, be-cause apparently, Patrick's a celebrity at the Seaside Beach Resort.

I spy Amar from the Shake and Bake and feel my face get even redder.

"Patrick, you clean up good," he calls from his table.

Ugh.

I shall never live down the Shake and Bake disaster.

A bunch of people from Fairfield Park are here wearing their striped amusement park T-shirts. "Fairfield Park's going to win tonight," a lady says. I think it's the one from the deep-fried Oreos. I can taste them at the back of my throat.

A guy gives his neighbor a high five. "Yes, Patrick's here! When're you calling the numbers?"

Patrick smiles. "We'll see if I get a chance."

He turns to me. "Calling numbers means that you get to announce the numbers to the room."

"Why does everyone want you to call?"

"Last week was my first time calling. I kind of messed it up and a whole lot of people won who shouldn't have. Now they want me to do it every week."

"Put Patrick on the mic!" someone says. The whole room laughs.

Patrick waves and smiles. There's not an ounce of redness on his face.

Finally, we reach the front of the room. Queen Bea's set up with a microphone at a podium, wearing a yellow-and-black-striped cardigan. Her beehive hair's so high, it practically touches the ceiling.

Two men count a bunch of numbered balls and dump them into a clear cylinder that spins in a continuous round.

"Number three," the man says.

"Number three, cup of tea," says the other man, as he checks something off a list.

"Number seventy-three."

"Seventy-three, queen bee," the other man says, again checking the list.

The crowd picks it up. "Queen Bea, Queen Bea, Queen Bea," they chant.

Queen Bea waves us over.

With tornado-like force, bingo balls spin in the plastic tube. The men check off two more balls and put them in the spinner. "That's it! We're ready to roll," says one.

Queen Bea taps the microphone. "Who's ready for

BINGO?" She wears a shirt that says *Grandma Is My Name and Bingo Is My Game* along with bright yellow reading glasses with little bees all over them.

The room erupts into applause.

"Queen Bea, roll us the winning numbers," Amar yells from his table.

She points at us. "You sit right here, Cora. And Patrick, no nonsense today. Just confirm the numbers on the cards, okay?" She smiles at me. "Is this your first time?"

I nod and ignore the heat beating in my face as we sit at a small table near the podium.

"Patrick will show you the ropes," she says with a strong pat of her hair. It wobbles a little.

Patrick hands me two bingo cards. "This is just for practice, since we didn't put any money in the pot. You won't win anything today." He hands me what looks like a really big purple marker. "Here's your dauber. All you do is stamp the numbers when my grandma calls them, and if you get a line of numbers in a row, you win. Bingo!" He says it like it's the easiest thing to do.

He pushes a little red admission ticket at me. "Queen Bea already bought us two tickets for the door prize raffle. Write your name on the back of this. They do a drawing at the end. Mrs. Gitney's in charge."

I spy Mrs. Gitney holding a basket wrapped in cellophane full of vitamins, Epsom salts, a smelly candle, and assorted licorices.

"Texas Blackout," Queen Bea says into the microphone—
all business.

Patrick explains. "If she calls an even number first, then
you try to get all the even numbers marked. If she calls an odd
number first, then you try to mark all the odd."

"One dozen," Queen Bea calls into the microphone.

The crowd murmurs as people daub their numbers.

I scan my cards. One dozen. One dozen what?

Patrick leans over. "Twelve. That's number twelve. You
have one right there." He points to it.

"Two little duckies."

Everyone daubs their cards.

"Oh, sorry, that's twenty-two." He searches mine. "You
don't have any."

"Why do they call twenty-two 'two little duckies'?" I ask.

"The numbers kind of look like two swimming ducks in
profile."

"Queen Bea," says Patrick. "Can you call the regular number too, for the beginners?"

She nods.

"So, you're fine now, right?" He stands. "I've got to go
around and check numbers and make sure your surprise is
ready."

I wish he'd stay. I do deep breathing and focus on the cards
in front of me.

"Nineteen, goodbye, teen." Daub.

"Sixty-two, tickety-boo." Daub. Daub.

"Sixteen, dancing queen." Daub. No daub.

"Seven, lucky." No daub. No daub.

But I watch Patrick out of the corner of my eye. People like him. They pat his arm, or head, and are always smiling at him. How does he manage to be friends with everyone?

Someone yells bingo, and the crowd groans. Then it all starts over again.

CHAPTER 33

14 Minutes Until I Meet the Detective

*P*atrick makes another pass by my table. "Are you ready to lose your mind?" He's so excited he might float to the ceiling.

I hesitate.

Brain says: You will not be losing me.

"You brought what we found at Cat's Cove, right?"

I nod and pat my pocket.

"Because he said you had to bring it."

My heart thumps. I didn't know I was meeting someone. I especially don't want to show my precious find to some stranger. "He who?" I ask.

"Hold on to your seat, because guess who's here?" Patrick bounces. "The guy who runs the blog *Nine Lives*!! Officer Bayless, the retired detective. He comes to bingo every week and said he'll look at what we found!"

Patrick's right, I do have to hold on to my seat. The retired investigator who knows everything about The Cat? The guy who's an expert on the plane crash, and the possible gold coins, wants to talk to me? I feel light-headed.

"Come on." Patrick takes my hand. I burn as I follow him through the maze of tables. We stop in front of a cranky-looking bald man with a very large mustache. His bingo cards are laid on the table in a severe, straight line.

"Here she is!" Patrick exclaims.

He turns to appraise me. "So, this is the treasurer hunter." He slides on his glasses and gives me a discerning look. Officer Bayless can see through to my soul.

Should I tell him I love his blog? Should I tell him my Cat theories? Should I show him my treasure? My ears throb with heat.

"All right, then." He places his dauber perpendicular to his cards. "Let's see whatcha got."

Patrick elbows me.

Officer Bayless's face doesn't crack. I think he has one mood—serious.

I tremble. What if he says it's nothing but junk? What if it has nothing to do with The Cat? Once I show him what I've found, I'll never be able to take it back.

Brain says: Don't share your precious find.

My stomach hurts.

Patrick says, "We found it down at Cat's Cove. You're going to love it, Officer. It's amazing!"

"We'll see." He eyes both of us, unconvinced.

Even Patrick's cheerful attitude can't melt the frosty Officer Bayless.

I pull the lock out of my pocket and place it on the table. His bingo cards bounce, falling out of line.

Officer Bayless picks it up, turning it every which way. He presses the center piece, which moves just a little. He pokes the three little holes on the side with the tip of his pen. He tries to pull the top of the lock off.

"We think it's something called an impossible lock," I croak, trying to use my outside voice. I wipe my sweaty hands on my pants. "I saw something like it on the internet."

"Hmmmm," he says.

He eyes the holes on the side. When he gets to the three scratch marks, he pauses. He takes off his glasses and polishes them. Then he pulls out a key ring that has a little magnifying glass attached to it and peers at the marks.

"Hah!" He slaps his leg.

"It's good, right?" asks Patrick.

Queen Bea booms over the speakers, "Patrick Borgwin. Calling Patrick. We need you at the podium pronto."

"Sheesh!" says Patrick. "I forgot I was checking bingo cards. Sorry, gotta go." He hurries off to do his job.

I take a deep breath and try to not think about my tomato face.

"Young lady, you've got yourself a bona fide Cat find, I swear." His face softens. "I'd bet my blog on it." He points to the back of the lock. "You see these three scratch marks? That's no accident. That's The Cat's—she marked everything important with three claw marks. They're all uniform scratches—like a monogram. Twenty-five years ago, her family showed this mark to us in case we found other items that belonged to her. They even hired their own private investigation team, who found nothing, I might add." He fiddles with the lock. "This could be from her case of coins."

"The coins are really real? Really *real*?" I can feel my eyes popping out of my head.

He nods. "Her family told us about those as well." He lowers his voice. "But I don't make that public knowledge." He hands the lock back to me.

Queen Bea says, "Seventy-three, Queen Bea."

The crowd chants, "Queen Bea, Queen Bea, Queen Bea."

"Herb, you watchin' my cards?" the detective asks his seatmate, his face all hard lines again. "Look, you missed number twenty right there."

Herb throws his hands in the air and laughs.

"Do you think . . . ?" I whisper-say.

Officer Bayless leans closer, his attention back on me. "Speak up, young lady. These darn speakers are so loud, I can't hear a thing."

I swallow. "Are you going to write about what I found? About Catherine Van Larr's lock on your blog?"

He looks at me, his gaze steady. "How about you and I keep this information to ourselves. We don't want people all the way from kingdom come here muddying the waters of La Quinta Beach. I myself enjoy a day of treasure hunting. Don't you?"

I nod.

"You don't mind if I throw my hat in the ring and get out to La Quinta Beach to look for the gold myself?"

"No," I say.

He holds out his hand. "May the best person win."

I shake it. "Deal."

Queen Bea's voice interrupts over the loudspeaker. "Get ready for Blackout."

Officer Bayless turns back to his bingo cards.

I peer down at the lock. The Cat held this in her hands? My stomach flutters.

I text Minny: I found something from The Cat!!!!!!

But then I don't send it.

I forgot she never responded to my forced friend question. I think I have my answer.

CHAPTER 34

3 Minutes and 5 Seconds Until My Forced Friend Likes Flowers

*P*atrick eats three brownies and two snickerdoodles while people put away the leftover desserts.

Queen Bea presses her forehead against mine. "I hope you caught the bingo bug tonight."

Normally, I don't even like people looking at me, let alone pressing their foreheads against mine, but I nod.

I think maybe Queen Bea gets me.

We unlock our bikes outside the Seaside Beach Resort.

"Can you put this in your basket?" I ask. Mrs. Gitney gave me a doggie bag full of brownies that I'm sure Sunshine will want to share.

Patrick throws it in, like it's a basketball.

"You're going to squish the frosting."

He smiles. He's got brownie in his teeth.

I pull the puzzle lock from my pocket and examine the claw marks. They do look made on purpose. They're so precise. I shiver.

La Quinta Beach is only five minutes from here.

Patrick and I ride our bikes side by side, down the middle of Castano Street. Patrick's old fuchsia beach cruiser whines loudly with each wheel rotation jiggling a basket covered in flowers. "Marbella gave me this bike totally free!" he says. "Can you believe it?"

"I can. Do you like the flowers?"

He makes a face. "Yeah, and the basket." My doggie bag bounces inside it. "Plus—" He jumps the curb. "This bike has great shocks!" He clunks onto the pavement, hard. His smile is so sheepdog. "I got like a foot off the ground!"

More like two inches, but I stop myself from saying it. Instead I say, "Officer Bayless said the lock belonged to The Cat." I smile.

"What?! Are you serious?! I knew it." He pumps his fist into the air.

I pump my fist into the air too. "Amazing, right?"

"So that means the treasure's down there!" Patrick jumps another curb.

"Probably. Wanna go down to Cat's Cove?" I ask, looking at my phone. It's exactly 6:03 P.M. I have twenty-seven minutes until Mom said I needed to be home. Now that we know for sure that we have a true Cat artifact, I want to examine where we found it again.

"I'm down." He slows. "Too bad you don't have your metal detector thing with you."

"Ruva."

"What?"

"That's its name—like how it sounds. RUUUUUVAAAH,"
I say.

He cocks his head. "Yeah, I hear it." He jumps a speed bump. "I should name my bike."

"Bessie," I say as I jump over the speed bump too.

He crinkles his nose. "How about TM2?"

"That's not a name."

"Short for Time Machine Two." He laughs. "Wouldn't it be awesome if I could ride this bike at the speed of light, and then time would bend, and then I could meet my mom and dad right now?! I wouldn't have to wait for the lunar eclipse on Monday."

My heart thumps. Patrick's time machine is fiction. Make-believe. Like—like Superman, or turning invisible, or . . . finding buried treasure.

My face heats up. Maybe all dreams sound impossible.

If I had a time machine, I know what I'd do. I'd go back to the exact moment Uncle Richie ran away and I'd fix everything. I'd save Vo's broken heart. Maybe I could stop him from taking Mom and Dad's money. I'd keep my baby self from falling out of the crib.

I touch the scar on the back of my head. If I could go back in time, Mom and Dad wouldn't fight about him. Or me. I'd have a normal brain.

Brain says: I am normal.

I think about Uncle Richie and Dad. And Mom and Aunt Janet. And Blue and Sunshine. Families are hard. "Why do you want to meet your parents so bad?" I ask Patrick. "You have Queen Bea."

Queen Bea seems easy compared to my family.

Patrick stops his bike at the train tracks. "Queen Bea always says things like, 'Patrick, you got that from your mom or this from your dad.' But I don't know that for sure. I need to meet them if I'm ever going to feel like myself." His voice cracks. "I want to know who I'm part of."

I nod. Even though I love my family, I don't know that I really feel a part of them. I'm never perfect enough.

Patrick clears his throat, his voice soft. "Queen Bea says the time machine is a fool's errand." He runs his hands through his hair and looks toward the cove.

"Either that or she doesn't like you using her credit card." I smile at him.

We wait as a train passes; the light fades in the distance.

"You're the only one who believes me," he says, his eyes earnest. "You believe I can do it, right, Cora?"

We walk our bikes over the tracks. I really, *really* want his time machine to work.

It takes me shorter than eight minutes to decide. "I'll do everything I can to help you, Patrick. I promise."

And that's not a lie.

We park our bikes at the top of the trail near Pacific Coast Highway and head down. The breeze stirs and I pull up my hood for added warmth. The smell of campfire lingers in the air. Clumps of dirt roll ahead of us on the path.

"Race you!" Patrick speeds ahead. He's electric again. I follow him, then trip on a boulder and land sprawled in the sand. Patrick turns back and fake trips too. He lands next to me with an "oof." We laugh.

I turn and look at the sky. A small planet glows brighter near the horizon. Dusk is almost gone. "Thanks for introducing me to Officer Bayless," I say. "That was really awesome of you . . . even if . . ." I hesitate—do I say it? "Even if the principal *made* you be my friend."

He sits up, choking on his spit. "Wait. What? The principal isn't making me be your friend." His dark eyes bore into mine. "The school counselor asked if I'd be interested in walking a student to and from class for a little bit. He told me it was you, and I was like, YESSS."

"Just walk me to class?"

He nods.

"And you wanted to?" He wasn't asked to be my forced friend?

"I mean, who wouldn't want to be friends with you? You've got a metal detector! And you're hilarious."

"I am?" My heart bumps in a maybe-I-believe-him way. "Thanks."

He's not my forced friend?

I can't help but think about Minny.

Patrick stands. "What was The Cat thinking when she flew over La Quinta Beach?" He looks up at the sky. "Do you think she planned it all? Was she trying to disappear forever? Was it an accident?"

"I don't know." I walk to the shoreline. "Help me find where we dug up the lock."

A cool breeze whips through the cove, making Patrick's hair dance.

"Right here?" I ask, counting ten paces aloud.

"Yeah, that looks good."

"Do you think The Cat's ghost roams the beach?" I ask. Here, tucked under the highway, it seems possible. The water barely ripples. It's the perfect place for haunting.

Patrick throws a large rock into the water and a huge splash ruins the quiet. "Nope. I don't believe in all that."

"I do," I say. Minny swears she saw the ghost cat one night at La Quinta Beach when her family had a bonfire. And what about what Mrs. Piedmont saw?

"Remember when I scared you bad?" He smiles his sheepdog smile.

"You didn't."

"You booked it out of here so fast with your metal detector."

I'm annoyed. "Well, you . . . you looked ridiculous with that crown thing on your head. You freaked me out."

"I know."

"What were you doing anyway?"

"Testing the air for humidity." Like it's so obvious. "On the night of the lunar eclipse, the precipitation has to be just right, or I won't be able to go back in time. It's a well-known fact that it's better to test humidity from the top of your head, since that's where time travel's initiated."

I make myself believe him. "Why was Ando here?"

"I told him I was running some important tests."

"Ando knows you're building a time machine?"

"Sure."

"Who else knows?"

"I don't know. I talk about it a lot, I mean, it *is* my passion."

We head up the hill toward our bikes. There's a light at the end of the jetty. It flashes in the newly created dimness. I can barely make out two people standing at the end of the jetty all in black—wet suits, I think.

"Should we go check it out?"

Patrick practically vibrates. He loves a good adventure. "Let's go," he says.

As we get close to the jetty, there are deep voices.

We reach the rocks. The lights glow from the front of the men's headlamps.

"I ordered those for the lunar eclipse," Patrick whispers loudly. "So you can free up your hands."

"Paulo," a voice says, "bring the boat closer. I've got one more tank to load. Do you have the masks?"

Paulo?

I trip on something and land hard on the jagged rocks. "Oof." My heart pounds.

"Are you okay?" asks Patrick.

I rub my knee; already I can tell I'll have a bruise.

I peer over the rocks to get a better look. It's Dad and Uncle Richie, prowling around the jetty. My dad, the guy who's supposed to be *my* treasure-hunting partner.

They get in the boat and rev the engine.

"Hey!" I yell, climbing up and over, but my shout is swallowed by the wind. They head out to the bay. If either one of them turns around, I can't tell.

"Where are they going?" Patrick asks.

"To the breakwater, I think. The artificial reef created from wrecked ships."

Patrick looks surprised. Finally, something I know that he doesn't.

"The Cat's plane is out there. And maybe her gold," I say.

The boat engine fades—there's only the sound of waves crashing.

1 2 3 4 5

I count the waves as they hit the jetty.

Brain says: Why didn't they invite you?

I do deep breathing.

"Who was that?" Patrick asks.

I pause. The wind whips my hoodie from my head and my hair swirls around my face. "Competition."

Minny hasn't responded to my texts in what feels like forever, but I check my phone again out of habit.

Minny texts: `I lost my phone bt mom jst fnd it whats a forced friend`

I text: `Did Mrs. Montgomery make you be my friend in second grade?`

My heart thumps. And for a second I wish I never asked

her that question. Little dots appear on the screen. They stop. They start again. They stop and don't return. Dad was right. My teacher made her.

I text again: You HAD to be my friend?!!!!

Minny texts: No.

Minny texts: Yes.

Minny texts: At first I did it bcuz Mrs. Montgomery askd me

My fingertips pulse.

I knew it.

Brain says: I told you.

Shut up, Brain.

Minny texts: But when I got to know u I wnted u 2 b my frind 4realssssss

My heart thumps.

In my mind, I see Patrick's toothy smile and wild hair. I'm glad the counselor asked him to walk me to class.

Minny texts: I SWEAR!!!!!

Maybe I'm glad Mrs. Montgomery asked Minny to be my friend.

I text: Really?

Minny texts: YES REALLYYYY

I text: Okay then.

CHAPTER 35

Sunday: 35 Minutes Until I Steal Patrick's Electrons

Queen Bea pokes her head into Patrick's bedroom. "You promise me you're not running away and joining the circus?" Her honeybee glasses perch on top of her gray beehive hairdo like a cherry on a sundae. Her wrinkles seem even more pronounced when she's worried. "This looks mighty suspicious."

"No, Grandma, I swear. We're just getting ready for tonight's run-through. The lunar eclipse is tomorrow night. We need to troubleshoot." He looks like he might combust; energy radiates from his body like a microwave on high.

I shove a tangle of wires into Patrick's duffel bag and wonder how this mess can actually create time travel. I pull out a plastic astronaut guy. "You want to bring this?"

"You mean Neil? He's my moral support."

First, we pack up Patrick's time travel stuff, where I'm his second. Then, we'll go to Cat's Cove to treasure hunt, where he'll be my second, and then we head to the pier to do the time travel run-through.

Patrick zips up the bag and hefts it over his shoulder and motions for me to do the same with mine. "Don't let Queen Bea see those car batteries," he says under his breath. "Amar's dropping them off later. I told him they're for my friend's dad."

"Whose?"

"Yours."

Outside, Queen Bea picks the dead blossoms from her plumeria bush. "I still wish you'd let me drive you over."

Patrick shakes his head. "We've got it covered." He straps his duffel bag to Marbella's bike. "If I'm going to travel through time, I better be able to lug all the gear myself."

I laugh, because I'm lugging the other half.

Queen Bea sighs and waves at Marbella, who's just opened her screen door. "Hello, there."

She waves back, then gives her hair a pat and sweeps imaginary dust off her porch.

"Okay, we're all set!" Patrick declares.

"We're all rooting for you, Patrick," Marbella says. There's silence and then a look passes between her and Queen Bea, which I recognize instantly. It's a look I know well: weirdo.

From his own grandma?

Queen Bea gives Patrick a big smooch on his cheek, which he promptly wipes off. "I wish you'd give this time machine stuff a little break, Patrick. You're working yourself into a frenzy."

He ignores her.

She picks off another dead bloom. "I suppose it's good to keep you busy." Another look passes between Queen Bea and Marbella.

My fingers shake as I bungee Patrick's bag onto the back of my bike. Something rises in me. "He's got to try, doesn't he?"

Marbella stops sweeping.

Queen Bea stops picking.

Even Patrick stands with his mouth open. My fingers clench into balls as heat rises through my body.

"Well, of course, dear," says Queen Bea. She pats Patrick's shoulder. "There's nothing wrong with a dream."

Marbella says, "Dreams—they make the world go around."

Neither one of them are convincing.

"It's going to work!" I half shout. "You'll see." Adrenaline pumps through my body. Now *I'm* electric. I throw my leg over my bike and perch there, like I've just proven everything.

"That's right!" Patrick pumps his fist into the air.

Queen Bea nods. "Fine. Fine. Bedtime's at nine, so you be back before then."

He grimaces and jumps onto his bike and we circle his driveway, around and around. "I'll be back by then to give you a lesson in time travel!" Patrick yells. We laugh like maniacs. We are maniacs. Time traveler and treasure hunter!

He points to me. "We're going to do it!"

We fly our bikes, weaving around cars and people at Cascade Springs by the Sea.

Someone says, "Watch it."

But we don't.

We zip past Wally with his walker and his slippers.

"Slow down," he says.

We fly faster.

"We're UNSTOPPABLE!" I yell, not letting people with eyeballs who stare as us bother me one bit. They stare and stare and stare. So, who cares about eyeballs?

We pass the WELCOME sign and the NO CHILDREN sign and give a thumbs-up to the scowling security guard.

"Walk those bikes!" he yells.

But we don't.

Patrick chants with me. "Un-stopp-able! Un-stopp-able!" We zoom through the streets of La Quinta, chanting louder and louder, until my throat feels raw. He's infected me with his protons and electrons.

Patrick's barky sheepdog laugh is endless. His bike whines over the speed bumps. Astronaut Neil Armstrong wobbles and almost tumbles out of Patrick's flowered basket. Our laughs mix together like toast and jam. Like peas and carrots. Like Taco Tuesday.

"We're amaziinnnnnnggggg!" he yells.

And in that moment, we are.

CHAPTER 36

1 Hour and 12 Minutes Until I Find Two More Treasure Hunters

*W*e stop at my house for my metal detector.

Patrick checks his watch. "Test run in three hours!" His big voice fills every empty space.

"Shhhh." My heart thumps. I don't want Mom-questions. Or Sunshine-bothering. "Okay," I say, checking the time. It's 4:24 P.M. "We have enough time to get over to Cat's Cove to concentrate on where we found the puzzle lock, and then if we don't find anything there, we'll spread out and focus on the south side, where most everything washes up."

"Roger that." He salutes me. "After that we'll do the run-through for the time machine."

"To being seconds," I say as I hold up my hand.

Patrick slaps it.

Yes, Brain. I give high fives now.

Brain says: Gross.

Dad's fishing boat is still gone. My chest tightens, but I push the thought away.

Ruva sits in the cabinet next to Dad's brand-new metal detector.

"Here," I say, showing Dad's to Patrick.

"Inspiring," he says, properly impressed. "My very own metal detector."

"My *dad's*. But you can use it for today. Just be super careful."

He nods—his hair bounces. "Cool. Cool. Cool." He pushes the red button. It hums.

"Shush," I say, handing Patrick my dad's headphones—the ones I got him for Christmas last year. He'd be mad if he knew I was letting Patrick use it. But it's his fault. Dad should be here with me. We should be doing this together.

"Are you okay?" Patrick asks.

"Of course. I know right where we should look for the treasure today."

"I shall follow your lead," he says. "I'm your faithful second."

Just as we strap our metal detectors to the backs of our bikes, the door opens from the kitchen to the garage. Out steps Sunshine, framed in a triangle of light.

"Cor-rah!" She folds her arms, exasperated.

"What?"

"Mom's been looking all over for you."

I tighten the bungee around Ruva. "No, she hasn't. I texted her that Patrick and I are going to Cat's Cove."

She appraises Patrick—his bike, his hair, his toothy

smile—clearly unimpressed. "Well, you promised you'd play Uno with me."

"I will," I say. "Tonight, when I get home."

She gives me her longest sigh because she has Patrick as her audience.

He rolls his bike over to her. "Hi there. What's your name again? Cora's little sister?"

She makes a face. "Sunshine."

"That's the best name I've ever heard." He holds his hand up for a high five.

She stares at his flowered basket.

"Did you know Saturn has fifty-three moons?" Patrick asks.

"So?"

"Or that sometimes Saturn's rings disappear completely?"

"Yeah, I already knew that."

Doubtful. I give her a look.

"Whose bike is that?" she asks, pointing to Marbella's basket with the plastic Neil Armstrong inside.

"Mine."

"That's for a girl."

Patrick pops a wheelie. "Who says?"

He has her there.

"Did you know that Saturn is what they call a *gas* giant?" he asks.

She stares.

"Boom!" Patrick jumps off his bike. It falls with a clatter.

Neil Armstrong goes spinning and comes to rest under a cabinet.

Sunshine smiles.

"Watch out, gas giant coming through. Boom!" Patrick falls onto the floor.

Then she laughs.

"Boom! Boom! Boom!" Patrick hops like a frog with each boom.

Sunshine copies him and the two of them hop around the garage, booming at each other. She's figured out they're practically the same person.

Mom comes out of the house. "I thought you left already."

Chevy pads behind her.

"We're trying," I say.

I kneel and rub Chevy's sides. "Hey, buddy boy. I love you, you big doggy you."

Patrick hops over. "Whoa, your dog is amazing!" He rubs behind Chevy's ears. "You're so lucky you have a dog. Cascade Springs doesn't allow pets."

"Hello, Patrick," Mom says, and waves a coffee cup in his direction.

Immediately he stands and shakes Mom's hand, not once, but twice. "So nice to see you again, Mrs. Altman. Cora and I are going to Cat's Cove for purely educational reasons. Officer Bayless said the lock we found was The Cat's, so we *have* to go back and look for the gold. You don't have to worry about a thing, because we're a team, and whatever we find today, we'll share evenly—" He can't stop talking.

Mom interrupts. "It's all okay. Don't worry, Patrick." She smiles at me. She thinks I hate all his talking, but I don't mind so much.

"Dad said he wants to talk to you," she says.

I shrug.

"Just relaying the message." She smiles into her cup. It's not often that I prefer Mom to Dad. But since my uncle kidnapped Dad's life, I like Mom.

"Let's go," I say to Patrick.

We head down the driveway, riding our bikes. Sunshine runs after us, gravel flicking up with each step. "I want to go!" she yells.

Chevy runs too, barking short, happy barks.

"Next time," I yell. "I promise."

Patrick rides no-hands. "Farewell, fellow gas giant. I shall never forget you."

Sunshine falls into a fit of giggles.

Mom waves. "Stay safe! Check your cell!"

I smile. Warmth fills my chest and then my whole body. I'm almost, sort of—happy.

We reach Cat's Cove in thirteen minutes and forty-two seconds. The clouds hang low and thick in the sky—the air sticky on my skin. The plants are damp and limp. We stand on the hill and survey the beach. Only a few people climb the rocks at the jetty.

I grab Ruva and gently place Dad's metal detector into Patrick's hands. "Be careful with it."

"Oof," he says. "It's heavier than it looks." He slides on his butt halfway down the trail, then jumps up, holding it high over his head. "Don't worry! I got it!" If Dad were here, he'd freak.

Patrick says, "This metal detector seems really high-tech. I don't know how to work it. Too bad your dad's not here."

"I know how to use it. Plus, my dad's too busy now that my uncle came back."

"Where was your uncle?"

"I don't know, he was just missing. Now he's at rehab. Dad has to spend all his time over there helping him."

"That's good, I guess. If I wasn't feeling well and had to do a hard thing, I'd want my friends and family there."

My heart bumps. But Uncle Richie stole from us, and he let me fall and hit my head, and now I have a talking Brain. How do you forgive someone who does all that?

"You're not happy he's home?"

"My dad's always gone—" I realize how babyish I sound. I look at his metal detector in Patrick's hands. The last time we went treasure hunting was just before Minny moved. Dad found an old rusted locket, its chain missing. "For you," he said, handing it to me. "Now you have my heart."

Dad jokes.

I'll find The Cat's treasure without Dad.

I examine the sand. "I think we found the lock right around here."

"I think so too," says Patrick.

I give him a quick lesson on how to use Dad's metal

detector. "You take the area to the left, Patrick. Up near the yucca plants," I say. "That way we'll cover more ground."

"Sure thing, boss." He slaps on the headphones. "Look at me, I look like you!" he says in a too-loud voice. "Can you hear me?"

I give him a thumbs-up.

He follows the curve of the water, farther up the beach.

I take the beach closer to the north side. Ruva's methodical beep is soothing.

Ruva beeps. I dig. A small metal bracelet. I stick it in my pocket.

I walk another few paces.

Ruva beeps. I dig. A rusty bolt. I put it in a bag I carry for trash. I think I'm getting too far away from where we found the lock. I turn and head toward Patrick.

He's up the beach a little, digging with his hands. "Was it here?" he asks. He has mud smudged across his forehead. His hair blows in the wind, reminding me of an ancient warrior. Patrick stops digging and walks up the embankment. "We're close, Cora. Come up here."

It wouldn't be this high. I climb to meet him. The wind rushes over me, my hair flat against my head. The embankment overlooks the boats docked on the other side of the harbor—I drop Ruva where I stand.

It's our fishing boat. Uncle Richie's sitting in the place I usually sit. Dad's nowhere to be seen.

"Hey!" I yell. "You!" My voice turns to gravel. Instantly, my body shakes.

His face changes into recognition as he pulls off his baseball cap, squinting into the sun. He waves.

I don't wave back. He's in *my* seat. "Where's Dad?" I yell.

Patrick joins me. "Yeah, where's Dad?!" He echoes my intensity. It's good to have a second.

"Cor-Bell!" Dad waves at me from the dock. I didn't see him there.

Patrick waves back.

I elbow him.

"What?" he asks.

"What're you doing up there? Come down, honey." Dad motions to me.

"No!" I kick a large rock down the side of the embankment. It rolls, gaining speed, and splashes into the water below.

"Stay there," Dad says. "I'm coming up." He jumps into the boat. In eleven seconds the sound of metal scrapes against the large boulders at the bottom of the embankment.

"Let's go," I say.

We grab our metal detectors and are on our bikes, just as Dad's head crests over the hill.

"Cora!" he yells.

He's made his choice. I won't go back now. Not for all The Unattainable Finds in the world.

CHAPTER 37

30 Minutes Until Amazing

*T*he pier glows in the soft sunlight. It's now 6:04 P.M. Patrick and I pause at the base of the beach trail, near the parking lot.

"Why didn't you wait for your dad?" He asks.

I shrug. "We were in a hurry."

We park our bikes near the gelato shop, which is still open. Sunday nights can still be busy at La Quinta Pier. Campfires dot the beach; people laugh and scream as they roast marshmallows. A ukulele plays in the distance. A baby cries.

"It looked like he really wanted to talk to you."

"I have my cell phone. So it's fine."

Guilt burns the back of my throat. The whole reason Patrick's building this time machine is so he can see his mom and dad. My dad's right here, and I don't want to talk to him. What could he possibly say that would make me feel better?

Patrick looks underneath the bench near the gelato shop. "Yes!" Two car batteries sit where they're supposed to be.

"Amar didn't fail us." He lugs one of the car batteries onto his hip. "Can you grab the other one?" he asks.

With a duffel bag and a battery, I follow Patrick up the trail.

"This run-through has to be perfect," Patrick says. "Tomorrow night the lunar eclipse will be at its optimal point at 9:04 P.M."

My phone beeps.

Dad texts: Cora we need to talk.

I text: No.

Dad texts: Cora where are you.

I text: Ask Mom.

I put my phone in my pocket.

Brain says: He wouldn't understand any of this.

A train whistle sounds in the breeze. The moon slowly shows its face, winking on the horizon, as I follow Patrick up the beach trail.

He stops and dumps his gear. "Let's start right here." He begins to unpack, sorting electrical cords in order of color. Blue. Yellow. Red.

I add my cords to his piles. It takes us three minutes and thirty-seven seconds.

He tries on his helmet/energy cap. His hair sticks out in the front and on the left side. The cap has a cord that's attached to his iPhone.

"What's that for?" I ask.

"It gives me a readout of air pressure and battery charge."

"Did you make all of this yourself?"

"Mostly, but I buy a lot online." He holds up the purple morph suit. "And this." He pulls his cap off and turns it inside out. It's covered in what look like little blue foam stickers. "These blue spaces combine the energy from the car batteries and the energy from my brain to propel me up to the worm-hole created by the eclipse."

"So, you're literally being propelled by brainpower," I say.

He smiles. "Yep, you can blame my big brain."

Brains can be blamed for a lot of things.

Brain says: All the best things.

Patrick stares at the sky; his face turns somber. "You and your dad can work it out, right?"

I shrug. "Yeah, probably."

"You will!" He gives me his best toothy smile, then pulls the purple space suit over his clothes. He tucks the bottoms of it into his socks.

I stifle a giggle.

"Let me ask you this: Do you love your dad?" Patrick asks.

"Of course."

"If you love him, then you have to talk to him. Every day I wish I could talk to my mom and dad."

My hearts thumps. My insides feel like when I fell off my bike and scraped up my knee—red and bloody—I didn't let anyone touch it. It sat like that for a day, until Mom said I had to let her clean it out because it was infected.

What's happening with Dad makes me feel infected all over again.

Patrick says, "I'd do anything to meet my mom and dad. Even this." He spreads his arms wide over the gear and the space suit and his cap, crown, and helmet. "And your dad's right here on the same planet. You've got to fix whatever it is."

A lump rises in the back of my throat as dusk closes in.

"Ta-da!" Patrick puts his hands on his hips—purple suit, cap, helmet, wire crown, headlamp, goggles, gloves, and coils of wire wrapped around his right arm. He's painted *AMAZING* across his chest. He turns around—Neil Armstrong's taped to the back of his helmet. He says, "Neil's got my back."

I laugh.

He leans down and pulls a bunch of cords from his duffel bag. "Let me show you how to attach these. We're going to go through it all until we both have it down perfectly."

Patrick's time machine has to work.

CHAPTER 38

24 Minutes Until I Try

*M*om picks us up at the pier. Patrick and I lug our bags and our bikes into the back of our car.

"Wow. You've got a lot of stuff," Mom says. "What's going on?"

Patrick raises his eyebrows and shakes his head.

"A science experiment for school," I say, swallowing the truth.

Brain says: Lie.

Patrick interjects, "It's a group project. We're studying the changes of the tide with the lunar eclipse tomorrow night."

Mom says, "Sounds interesting."

After we drop Patrick off, Mom pulls into our driveway.

"Did you eat?" she asks.

I shake my head. "I'm not hungry."

"You sure?"

"I'm tired."

After I put my metal detectors and bike away, I walk to my

room and flop on the bed. Chevy jumps up and snuggles in with me.

Sunshine stands in my doorway, clinging to the frame. "Where's Patrick?"

"At home."

"I like him." She smiles shyly. "He's fun." She swings her body back and forth, holding on to the frame.

"Just like you."

Sunshine smiles wider. "And you too."

I'm fun?

"Come here." I pull her onto my bed. It only takes twenty-four seconds until we have wrestle mania.

Sunshine bounces on my bed. "Watch out, I'm a gas giant!" She makes farting noises on her bare arm and then collapses into giggles. Chevy yips and barks and tugs on my sleeve.

I wrap Sunshine in my blanket like a baby burrito. "I've got you, gas giant!"

Then I let Chevy lick her face to death.

"Nooo," she protests. But when I try to unwrap her, she complains even louder. Our laughs spin over our heads, mixing in with our protons and electrons. Each laugh brighter than the next, until I squint because of all the happiness. Sunshine's sunlight is showing.

And so is mine.

That night, after Sunshine and I have gone to sleep, I lie in bed and stare at the cracks in my ceiling. My door creaks open. A beam of light slides across my floor until it lands at my feet.

"Cora." Dad takes a step inside. "Cora, are you awake?" he whispers.

I make my eyes tiny slits so they look closed, but I can still see him. My heart pounds in my ears.

He stands at the foot of my bed and gently touches my foot. "Cor-Bell."

I pretend to sleep, but the blankets are suffocating.

He stands there for eight seconds, watching me pretend-sleep. Finally, he turns away.

Good.

My heart bumps. I take a huge gulp of air. But the bowling ball is back, squishing my stomach. Nothing feels good about ignoring Dad.

He places his hand on the doorknob and backs out, slowly, like a sand crab. He closes the door; the light follows him inch by inch, until it's almost black.

I take a deep breath. "Dad," I whisper-say.

He turns. The glow follows him back in, silhouetted by the light from the hallway. "I thought you were asleep."

"I'm not."

He sits on the edge of my bed. "I'm sorry."

I don't respond.

"I'm sorry I haven't been spending enough time with you lately. I've been with Uncle Richie and ignoring Mom and Sunshine and especially you."

I sit up.

"Since the moment I got the call from Richie on Saturday night to come and pick him up, I've thought about hardly anything else. I've been consumed with getting him better. I'm sorry I've been distracted."

I nod. "Okay."

He pats my hand. "Okay then. I was thinking, how about we go treasure hunting tomorrow after school? We haven't done that in a while. Around four o'clock?"

I should be happy. Dad—my dad—wants to treasure hunt. A week ago, I would've jumped at the chance. But now all I want to do is make an excuse. "I can't. Patrick and I are doing our—our science experiment tomorrow after school. I promised I'd help him."

Dad nods. "Oh yeah. Of course." His mouth smiles but it doesn't reach his eyes. "I understand."

I feel like I'm letting both of us down.

"How's Uncle Richie?" I ask.

"To be honest, not so great. Tonight he wanted to leave rehab."

"Why?"

Dad's shoulders slump. "Because getting over an addiction is really hard. Trying to be your best self, well . . ." He sighs. "Sometimes it can feel impossible."

That I know. "Is he going to stay?"

"He agreed to give it another try."

I almost reach out and pat Dad on the back, but then I remember I supposed to be mad at him. But something inside me softens a little.

The alarm on his watch chirps. "How about we go treasure hunting tomorrow morning, before school? Remember how we used to go early, at sunrise? Before Mom and Sunshine got up?"

I do remember—we did that back before I started middle school. That was only in fifth grade. Only before the summer. It feels like a whole different person ago. Slowly I nod. "Okay," I say. "Let's do it."

Dad stands. "Really? Great. It'll be just like old times. I'll wake you at six A.M."

I give him a thumbs-up—but I have so many questions. How can he forgive when Uncle Richie stole from our family? And why doesn't he care that it's Uncle Richie's fault that I fell, and my brain is broken? And how can he look for The Unattainable Find with his brother and leave me on my own?

Jealousy burns at the back of my throat. The bowling ball sits in my stomach.

How can it ever be like it was?

CHAPTER 39

Monday: 44 Minutes Until I Make a New Old Friend

*T*he morning light touches our driveway like it's been painted with Sunshine's watercolor brushes—the pastel shades splatter here and there.

Dad loads our metal detectors into the back of the VW van.

We get in and I pull my hoodie tighter against the crisp, fresh air. Normally, I love this—treasure hunting with Dad. But not today.

He starts the van and backs up on the driveway. "You tired?" he asks, looking sideways at me. I don't think we've been alone like this since the day he dropped me off at school and I ran away.

I shrug and stare at our front walk. The same walk where Mom and Dad carried Uncle Richie only ten days ago. Sunshine will be sad when she wakes up and sees we're gone.

The vintage van exaggerates every bump and turn as we head toward Cat's Cove. I sense Dad glance in my direction, but I try not to look at him. If I do, he'll see the questions I'm afraid to ask.

He clears his throat. "Was this not a good idea?"

I stare out the window.

"Are you not talking to me? Should we go back?"

1 2 3 4

I count the thin lines on the glove box.

Finally, I mumble, "It's fine."

He tries again. "What did you find at the cove the other day?" He turns right on Mission. The ocean sits dark and gray, not yet touched by the sun. I'm grateful to have something to stare at instead of not-Dad.

"I don't want to talk about it," I say.

Dad starts to say something, but then stops. He pulls into a parking space along Pacific Coast Highway, where we always park when we look for treasure.

Numbers tick off in my head. The ride has taken eight minutes, the same amount of time I didn't breathe when I was born. Birth asphyxia. I used to think those were the eight minutes that changed me. But now I know better. It was Uncle Richie.

"How come you let Uncle Richie come back?" I say, staring at the beach.

"Pardon me?"

"How can you forgive him, especially after what he did to our family?" My eyes feel as steely as the water.

Dad takes the keys out of the ignition, then he smiles. "Cor-Bell, it was just money."

I turn to him. "Not just money." Heat courses up my neck. "What about *me*? He was supposed to watch me. It's because of him that I fell out of my crib and hit my head."

Dad's face sobers.

"He's the reason I have anxiety and a talking Brain. I always thought it was because I didn't breathe for eight minutes when I was born, but it's *his* fault." My voice shakes.

Now it's Dad's turn to stare at the ocean.

"Cora, that's not true. Your fall when you were a baby was an accident. It could've happened with your mom or me at home. But you're right, Uncle Richie should've been there. That was his mistake." He places his hand gently on my head. "Believe me when I say that there is no connection between your anxiety and your fall when you were a baby. You are healthy."

I shake my head. "Then why does Dr. Rosenthal want me to take medicine?"

"Cora, you have anxiety. It's just a part of you. Like your brown hair and your intelligence and your good heart. You got some of those traits from Mom, and some from me, and some of it is just *you*. Medicine might help you feel less anxious, but we don't know for sure. You're not the first person in our family to struggle."

My talking Brain isn't because Uncle Richie let me fall? There are other people in our family who have talking Brains like me? I slide closer to him, wanting to believe.

I watch the gulls fight over a bag of chips someone left from the day before on the sidewalk.

"Who else has anxiety?" I ask.

Dad looks at me. "Well, I now know my brother has been struggling on his own for a very long time. He's learned through treatment that he may have been self-medicating, which led to his addiction to alcohol."

Uncle Richie?

"Don't you think he has waited long enough for forgiveness? It's been years and years. He's lived with the guilt and the stress and the worry. He's back making restitution. He wants to be a part of our family again." He turns and looks me straight in my eyes. "And I, for one, think it's time we let him."

My heart bumps.

I can't help but think about Blue and his fall while I was babysitting. About the guilt I feel. I wouldn't want it hanging over me for years.

Dad gives me a hug and then looks at his phone. "Do we still have time to treasure hunt?"

"The Cat's treasure is really important to you, isn't it?" I ask.

Dad gives me a funny look. "I look for treasure because I want to spend time with you. You're who I care about, Cora. When we treasure hunt, I get alone-time with my favorite firstborn. Didn't you know that?" He grabs my knee and squeezes it.

I shake my head. "Then why are you trying to find The Cat's treasure with Uncle Richie?"

He scrunches his eyebrows. "When?"

"I saw you at the jetty in the boat, and then at the harbor too. If you're not looking for the treasure, what are you doing?"

"Richie likes to dive. At his new rehab, they want their patients to resume old hobbies—to focus on what they love, and he likes nature. Being outside is a good distraction from the alcohol."

My heart squeezes.

Dad's not looking for the treasure with Richie? Dad wants to be with me?

I touch the scar on my head—a reminder of an accident from long ago, nothing more. Not a threat. Just a part of me.

The sunlight creeps over the water, illuminating a brilliant stream of bright across the ocean, a direct path to the cove.

A man walks past our van, in the direction of the jetty. I squint. The slope of his shoulders and his scowl are so familiar. Officer Bayless!

I unroll the window. "Hi!" I yell.

He turns around, pauses for a second, and then waves at me. "The early bird catches the worm!"

I say, "It sure does."

After we get our metal detectors out of the car, Dad puts his arm around me. "So, are we doing this?"

I nod. "Are you sure you don't care a bit about The Cat's treasure?"

He acts as if he's thinking hard, fist under his chin. "Well, I suppose if we stumbled upon it, then that would be nice."

I pull the lock out of my pocket. "How'd you like to hear a good story?"

CHAPTER 40

47 Minutes Until Time Travel Is Eclipsed

*P*atrick texts me: `Meet you at the pier at 8:45`
`lunar eclipse 9:04`

I text: `Your second is ready.`

La Quinta Beach is packed tonight. Mom drops me off at the pier so she can find a parking space.

Mrs. Sanderson, my English teacher, is giving thirty extra-credit points if we watch and write about the eclipse. It feels like the whole sixth grade and their families are here.

A sliver of a shadow covers the moon. A murmur rises from the gathering crowd. It's now 8:50 P.M. The lunar eclipse is about to begin.

I meet Patrick at the bait shop. "Finally," he says. His face is grim. His hair bigger than ever. It sways in the dark night as he vibrates with a nervous energy.

"Are you okay?" I ask.

"Of course. Why wouldn't I be?" Patrick plows through

the crowd toward the north side of the beach, where we can get on the trail.

I run to keep up with him. For once, he doesn't say hello to anyone, even though I recognize people from school. There's Sariah and googly-eyed Jocelyn from biology class. I keep my eyes on Patrick and hope to be ignored.

"Let me help you." I grab the handle of his duffel.

But he pulls it away. "I'm fine, Cora. What time is it?"

"8:54 P.M."

"Hurry, let's go."

I run with Patrick past the palm trees lining the beach trail—their fronds sway in the breeze, casting shadows like something out of a Dr. Seuss book.

Just after we cross the train tracks, the gate lowers, blaring bells and lights. After thirty-two seconds, a train rumbles past. People inside press their faces against the glass, hoping to get a glimpse of the transforming moon.

Bottle rockets shoot up from the beach, spraying light across the sky, and even though it's October, it feels like the Fourth of July. I try not to notice that there are so many people. It's starting to feel like Fairfield Park.

I take a deep breath.

Everything's fine.

Brain says: This is ridiculous.

A lady sells glow-stick necklaces, two for a dollar. Someone else sells glow-stick Rocket Copters. Flashes of neon zig through the dark night like shooting stars.

"This way," Patrick says, heading left on the beach trail.

I follow him for ten yards until he stops and crawls into the bushes. "They're still here!" He lugs out the car batteries we stashed last night. We turn on our headlamps to see better. The sounds of the crowd disappear behind us.

Patrick rummages through his duffel bag and pulls out his metal crown and places it on his head. He checks the reading on his phone and takes three giant steps to the right of the path and stands in the brush.

"What do you want me to do?" I ask.

"Get the cords ready." His face is tight with worry.

Ahead of us, the trail leads over the train tracks, past a clump of oleander bushes. The waves crash in the distance. Music plays from the deejay at the pier.

I look up. The bottom of the moon inches into shadow.

The lunar eclipse is beginning.

I shiver, half expecting the ghost cat to appear. I untangle the cords and lay them the way Patrick showed me last night, but I can't remember the exact order. I'm nervous for him. "Tell me again how the night will go."

"When I give you the sign, plug these wires into the top of the car batteries." Patrick shows me the order I should clip the wires into the car batteries. "Then you plug them into my suit. Six ports here on the back and six ports here on my cap. The cap will be on my head, but they're easy to clip. And then that's it."

I watch him intently. Each cord connects to a sticky pad, attached to the back of his space suit and to his cap underneath his crown. Patrick pulls his iPhone from the holster around his waist and checks it. He says softly, "Any second now I'll be going back in time to see my mom and dad."

My chest feels tight. Standing here under the transforming moon, time travel feels more real—more dangerous. "Are you sure it's okay to attach yourself to a car battery?" I ask.

He waves me away. "Of course."

"But we didn't hook you up last night. What if you get electrocuted or something?"

"It's totally safe." His jaw tightens.

It is? My heart begins to thud. I want to believe him, but I don't want Patrick to get hurt.

"I've been careful and built everything myself. It's safe!" His voice cracks on the last word. I've never seen him like this.

I take a big gulp of cold air.

"I need my second, Cora." His face is fierce. "Are you in or are you out?"

I can't let Patrick down. He needs me. No one ever needs me and it feels good. "I'm in."

The color comes back to Patrick's face. He hands me the red cable, then squints at his phone, muttering, "I swear, the readings were perfect last night, now they're a few degrees off—" He takes a step away from me.

Two people wearing neon necklaces walk toward us. I shine my flashlight at them and groan. Ando and Humberto. I step off the path so they can get by, but instead they stop.

"How's it going?" Ando asks.

My heartbeat bounces near my eardrums. I beg the heat from my face to go away.

"Nice hat." Humberto flicks Patrick's crown. The wires bounce violently as it slips to one side.

Patrick jerks out of his reach. "This is highly sensitive equipment. You're messing up the reading."

"Oh, okay," Humberto says sarcastically, elbowing Ando.

I want to slap off the stupid neon necklace wrapped around his head. *Don't touch Patrick.*

"Dude, chill," says Ando. Then he looks at Patrick. "How much time is left?"

Patrick says, "Three minutes, seven seconds until optimum alignment."

Ando nods at the duffel bag. "Is this it?" He reaches for the bags.

"What do you think you're doing?" I ask.

Ando's eyes open wide in surprise. Patrick looks up from his phone. "It's okay, Cora. I told Ando he could come and observe. You know, it's all hands on deck where experiments are concerned."

I shake my head. Ando doesn't know what he's doing. This is not the time for all hands on deck.

Humberto smirks at me.

I stammer, "But *I'm* your second. I'm your number two."

"That sounds like a personal problem," Humberto says. "I saw some porta potties down that way."

I spin around. "Shut up!"

Humberto clenches his fists but says nothing.

"Cora, you *are* my second," says Patrick. "But it's cool if these guys watch." He pats my shoulder.

Ando holds up his phone. "I can video."

Patrick looks up at the moon, almost half covered in shadow. "Cripes. Guys, come on." He zips open the duffels and starts throwing things out. "Hurry!" He takes off his metal crown and slips on the purple space suit over his clothes.

"Here," I say, handing Ando a flashlight. "Shine it there." I point it to Patrick's gear. So now, I guess, Ando is Patrick's number three. He hands it to Humberto.

I arrange the cords along the dirt path next to the batteries; each cord is seven feet long. "Ready," I say.

Patrick's suited up from head to toe. Cap, crown, space suit, Neil Armstrong, wires, holster, gloves, and goggles. Humberto bursts out laughing.

Patrick looks crazy. But still, he's my friend.

"What a freak," Humberto says, and looks to Ando for agreement.

Ando shakes his head. "Get out of here."

"Me? You'd rather hang with Freak One and Freak Two instead of me?"

Ando nods. "You're being a jerk."

Humberto chucks the flashlight onto the ground. The light disappears as it makes a cracking sound. He stomps down the path toward the pier.

Patrick says, "We kind of needed that flashlight."

I tap my headlamp. "We still have my headlamp and yours."

"Sorry about him." Ando brushes his hair away from his face.

Patrick yanks on the cord in my hands. "Hurry, attach this." He turns around. "Time?" he asks.

I say, "One minute, forty-five seconds." The moon is almost entirely covered—the trail darker than before.

"Hurry, Cora," says Patrick. "Attach the cords."

One. *Clip.*

Two. *Clip.*

Quickly I attach them. But with each clip, the bowling ball in my stomach gets heavier and heavier. Is this going to hurt Patrick? What am I really helping him to do? I pause my clipping. "Are you sure you're ready for this?"

Patrick's body trembles.

"Yeah, yes. Of course. Come on!"

We both glance at the sky. The eclipse is almost complete.

"Hold still," I say.

"Is it on?"

A cord falls to the ground. The ones connected to his back are fine, but a cap connection is loose. I fiddle with it, but it's so dark I can hardly see.

Ando shines his cell phone light until I find it.

Patrick shakes his legs out, like he's ready to jump off a high dive.

I examine the connection. A tiny bit of relief floods over me. "It's broken," I say.

"Cora, fix it!"

I push harder, trying to force the snap onto his cap, when Patrick pulls it off his head. He groans. "It worked perfectly yesterday."

"Here, let me try," says Ando. He fiddles with it as I take the phone camera from him. A timer runs on the screen.

"Fifty-seven seconds," I say.

In the distance, a train whistle blows.

"Let me see if I can find the other cap." I search through the duffel bags. Patrick has two of everything.

The moon is almost completely covered by the shadow of the earth. All three bodies align themselves in outer space, pushed and pulled by the gravitational fields of one another. Tension makes them perfect company, like peas and carrots, and toast and jam. Like friends—all working together to create the lunar eclipse phenomenon. Even with my headlamp on, the night feels as dark as the deep ocean.

Patrick crouches and covers his face. "We don't have time."

I hate to seem so defeated. "We do!" I hand Ando the camera again and then pull the extra cap over Patrick's head. "Forty-five seconds," Ando says.

The train blows its whistle again. The guard gates begin to drop, the flashing lights blinding.

"Come on, Patrick. You're going to go see your mom and dad." I pull him up by his arm and reach to rebuckle his helmet, but he jerks away.

The whistle comes closer and closer.

"Take those cords," he yells. "Attach them to the second battery. That should give me enough power to shoot me up into the wormhole."

The train rolls toward us. Patrick is twelve paces from the tracks.

"But we've never tested it with two batteries," I yell over the noise.

"It doesn't matter. It will give me the power I need. Cora, please!"

Only a tiny sliver of the moon is left. I press the cords to my chest. I can't do it. Sometimes being a friend means protecting those you care about.

"Patrick, get back!" I yell.

The train is almost upon us.

"Three seconds!" yells Ando. "Do it, Cora!" His face glows an eerie green, a reflection from the neon necklace wrapped around his forehead.

"I need my second!" Patrick screams over the blaring train whistle. His purple suit reflects the light shining from my headlamp. He glows from head to foot—his arms raised in triumph. The word he painted yesterday, *AMAZING*, emblazoned across his chest. "Attach them now!"

"I can't hurt you, Patrick!" I yell. Maybe being a friend is knowing when they need you to say no. Even when it's hard.

Patrick turns and grabs the cords from me and attaches them to the second battery himself.

The moon goes black. The ground rumbles. The whistle sounds just as the train passes. Wind washes over me. Electricity pops. Sparks shoot from the batteries like a small fireworks display.

I look to the sky. The moon has disappeared. I hold my breath. "Patrick?" I yell. But there's no answer.

Brain says: You killed him.

No, Brain.

Brain says: This is what happens when you help.

After what feels like forever, a beam of light escapes from the other side of the moon. The planets are out of balance. The gravitational pull is back to normal. Is Patrick up there? Is he in the stars? Is he with his mom and dad?

I trip over something on the ground and land with a thud, my hand trapped underneath my stomach. "Ouch!" I say. My hand throbs. I clutch it to my chest—why is it getting harder to breathe?

Breathe. Breathe.

Brain says: It doesn't matter if you breathe.

I search the sky. The stars, I attempt to count them, but my eyes won't focus.

Brain says: You can count forever, but you'll still be you.

I try to stand but then lie back down in the dirt. Everything feels cold. I try to ignore the large hand closing around my lungs and the white light swimming before my eyes. I do deep breathing, but nothing helps.

No. Not now. Not this. I'm Patrick's second. I can't have a panic attack.

"Cora!" Ando yells.

Brain says: I told you you'd fail.

Brain says: These friends aren't real. I'm real.

Brain says: I'm the only one who cares about you.

Squeezing my eyes tight, I ignore the throbbing in my hand. I roll to my side and try to sit up. But I can't. I lie there, frozen. My lungs squeezed tight. My air all sucked out.

Brain says: You're worthless.

Brain says: You can't help anyone. Not even yourself.

No. I take three deep breaths.

No, Brain. You're not the boss of me.

Brain says: I'm the only one who should be the boss of you. You don't know what you want.

I do know what I want. I want friends. I want to be okay.

My heartbeat slows. My eyes flick open—the eclipse continues. The shadow across the moon, still traveling slowly, slowly, finally reveals the brilliant light shining underneath.

I breathe.

I'm in charge, Brain.

1 2 3

I count the stars.

I'm not the same.

Ando stands over me, holding out his hand. "Come on." He pulls me to my feet, and I let him. Because that's what friends are supposed to do.

"Where's Patrick?" I ask. And then I see him lying on the ground next to me.

CHAPTER 41

6 Minutes and 12 Seconds Until the Lady

The train slows. A horrible squealing resonates from the tracks. The engineer must have seen the sparks from our batteries. Voices echo behind us on the beach trail.

Patrick lies on the ground completely still. His crown lies in the dirt next to him, the car batteries tipped on their sides.

I put my hand on his chest. "He's breathing," I tell Ando.

"Patrick." Gently, I shake him.

1 2 3 4

I count his breaths. Finally, he moans.

The left side of his space suit clings to his body, like Saran Wrap. When I touch it, it falls apart in my fingers. I tear the suit from him. His clothes underneath are fine.

"Patrick, are you okay?" I shake him again. He opens his eyes and nods.

"We've got to get out of here. People are coming," I tell Ando. "Get the stuff."

The batteries and cords will just have to stay. Ando grabs the duffels and our gear. He helps me pull up Patrick.

Patrick stands, dazed. He stumbles.

"Can you walk?" I ask.

"I think so."

"This way." I hook my arm through his and ignore the pain in my hand.

"What's going on?" Patrick asks, his eyes glassy.

A wind whooshes through the trail as the moon casts an eerie light on all of us. The bushes shudder, the breeze thick with salt. Suddenly, something moves ahead of us in the darkness. Goose bumps spread across my arms. The ghost cat?

"Ando! Watch out."

He sees it, and then it's the shape of a person. It *is* a person.

Adrenaline courses through my veins as I pull Patrick toward me. I want sunlight—a thousand minutes of sunlight. If the sun could shine down right now, then we'd be fine. We could recharge all our protons and electrons.

⏱

"Are you okay?" a woman asks. The clink of metal taps the ground. She steps closer, lingering for a moment. Why is that sound so familiar? An old lady steps into the thin moonlight and I realize—it's the lady who collects plastic bottles, the one with the tap shoes.

"We need to get out of here," I say. "He fell."

"Does your neck or back hurt?"

Patrick shakes his head no.

"Come with me." She puts her arms around Patrick and he clings to her.

People are coming. Their voices get louder. "Who's there?" someone calls. Flashlights bounce over the trail like sand fleas.

"Follow me," she says. Patrick leans on the tap shoe lady. She's stronger than she looks.

We follow her up the trail into the dark, away from the train, away from the jetty, away from the people. We follow her to wherever she wants to take us because any place is better than here.

She turns off the path, up to the top of the embankment.

"Where are we going?" Ando sounds worried.

She points. "Not far. Come." Her voice is fairy-like, a tap shoe fairy flitting over the beach in her overalls and bandanna. She opens a small gate and leads us to a little patio perched in front of an ancient house. The porch light casts sharp aloe vera–like shadows across the bricks. "Come sit."

Patrick coughs.

"Are you okay?" I ask.

Ando bumps my arm as he walks past.

"Ouch," I say. My hand still hurts.

The tap shoe lady opens the door to the house; light splashes across the grass. She points to a bench and Patrick sits. He mumbles something, but I can't make out what. I jiggle him. "Patrick, it's me, Cora."

He smiles dumbly.

"Patrick." Ando slaps his cheek. "Snap out of it."

"Stop it," I say.

Patrick touches his cheek but doesn't look offended.

"You fell pretty hard." I squint at his singed head. "Did you get electrocuted? It happened so fast."

"I have it all on video." Ando holds up his phone.

Patrick's eyes go wide. "I'm back," he half whispers as he rubs his neck.

"You never left," I reply.

He bolts up and laughs his big sheepdog laugh.

Relief washes over me. The world needs a Patrick. I need Patrick. "You might have a concussion." I point to the bench. "Sit down."

But he doesn't. He's too amped. He breaks into a huge toothy smile. "Wow, you guys look exactly the same."

I nod. "You were only knocked out for a few seconds."

Patrick claps his hands and looks at the sky. The moon shines back, large and bright. A small crescent-shaped shadow takes a bite out of the right corner. "I did it!" he exclaims. "I can't believe I did it!" His hair stands on end. "Woo-hoo!" He runs a circle around the patch of grass in front of the little house.

"What are you talking about?" Ando asks, waving his phone around.

"I WENT BACK IN TIME!" He pumps his fist into the air. "Yes! I knew it would work." He does a weird little shuffle dance.

Ando and I stare at him.

Brain says: Did I miss it?

"You were with us the whole time," I tell him. "You didn't go anywhere."

"I went back. I saw my mom and dad. I saw Queen Bea, except her hair was brown."

"No, Patrick. You hit your head. You were dreaming."

His eyes glisten as he grabs my hand. "Cora, I saw my dad. I saw my mom. They were scuba diving. They put their arms around me and told me they were proud. They said they loved me." He hesitates. "They're really cool."

I feel myself shaking my head at him, but I swallow the words that go with my head shake.

"Should we call your parents?" the tap shoe lady asks, her voice high and sweet.

A black cat curls around her feet. *Meow.*

"We will. I have my cell phone." I pull it out, but Patrick grabs my shoulder.

"I'm a time traveler, Cora." He holds up his hand for a high five. He looks so happy. But I can't high-five him, not when I know it's not true.

His hand hovers in the air, waiting for mine. Finally, I place my good hand up to his, a mirror of his own—warm. Cozy.

Ando puts his phone in his pocket. "I texted my dad. He's coming to get us."

"But my mom can—" I stop. How am I going to explain this to her? My left hand hurts, my clothes are filthy, and I don't know what to say about Patrick's time travel.

"Thanks, Ando. That's really nice of you."

I text Mom: Ando Mendez's dad is bringing us home. Be home in twenty.

Mom says: Sunshine and I are leaving now. Are you sure you don't want to come home with us?

I text Mom: In car already.

The tap shoe lady hands me a cup of something hot. She looks like she might blow away.

I shake my head no.

She hands Ando my cup.

"Thanks." He takes a sip. "Is this chamomile?"

She nods.

He takes a large gulp. "My mom makes me this when I can't sleep." He lifts his chin to finish the tea and his hair falls back. His earring glints in the moonlight. Then Bernando Mendez smiles with those straight white teeth.

I look away.

For being the king of everything, Ando's nothing like what I thought he'd be.

The tap shoe lady stands there, waiting.

"Thank you." I say to her. I never would have imagined that she could help me the day I met her at IHOP. "Really, that was super nice of you."

She looks down at her tap shoes. "You're welcome."

"My dad's here." Ando texts something on his phone, then he gathers a duffel bag and holds one out to me.

I take it and slip my arm through Patrick's, but he pulls away. "I'm fine," he says. "Time travel's good for me. I've never felt better."

"I guess, see you later," I say to the lady.

I follow along the stepping-stones and we let ourselves out the side gate. A car waits for us on the street.

Ando flings open the back of the car and throws in a duffel bag. I throw mine in too.

"Wow, you guys have a lot of baggage," Ando's dad says, and laughs at his own dad joke. Patrick laughs too.

Ando's in the front seat and Patrick and I are in the back. So, this is what it's like to be in the king of everything's dad's car.

"Whew, you smell like campfire," says Ando's dad. "Where's Humberto?" Ando and his dad look a lot alike—his dad has long hair and an earring too.

"He went home with someone else." If his dad thinks this is weird, he doesn't say anything.

I examine Patrick more closely. Bits of his hair are burned and he's covered in trail dust. A huge smudge streaks across his forehead. I'm glad it's dark so Ando's dad doesn't notice.

"How was the eclipse?" Mr. Mendez asks.

Ando hesitates. Finally he says, "Educational."

I say, "Scary."

"AMAZING," Patrick says. We drive down the road, away from the tap shoe lady's house, and La Quinta Beach, and the train. Away from . . . time travel?

"Tell me about the eclipse." Ando's dad turns the car left on Mission.

Ando, Patrick, and I look at one another and burst out laughing. How do you explain one of the craziest nights of your life?

"I'll tell you later, Dad."

Patrick stares out the window, his eyes fixed on the moon, a huge smile spread across his face. "Amazing," he says again.

Ando turns around in his seat and looks me right in the eyes. He smiles.

Brain says: If he really knew you, he wouldn't smile like that.

It's suffocating in here. The car bumps and we pause at a stoplight. I pull my hoodie up and look down at my feet.

Brain says: Secretly, everyone hates you.

No, Brain. NO.

I ride the Shake and Bake. I play bingo with Queen Bea. I talk to Officer Bayless. I find treasure. I use a cell phone. I tell Dad how I feel. I'm Patrick's second. I ride in Ando Mendez's car and—

I pull my hoodie from my head and look back at Ando.

I'm happy, Brain.

For once, I don't turn into a human tomato. Instead I smile, with my teeth showing—a real smile. A Patrick-smile.

You can stay, Brain, but I'm in charge.

CHAPTER 42

Tuesday: 1 Hour and 12 Minutes Until We Are a Family

*T*he next morning, the doctor's office is cold, the light flat. We've been here a total of sixty-five minutes. After Advil and icing my hand on and off all night, Dad said he thought it might be broken. He was right. The doctor says it's a hairline fracture. The nurse has the X-ray up on the monitor.

"See it right there?" Mom says to Sunshine. "Do you see that line? That's the break."

Sunshine squints. "It doesn't look broken to me."

I wince as the nurse presses a bit of fiberglass tape over my cotton-covered hand. She wraps it around and around and then smooths it. My new neon cast glows.

"That should take at least thirty minutes to dry," the nurse says.

Sunshine flexes her hand. "Why can't I get a cast? Just a little one."

The nurse laughs. "You think you want one now, but after a day you'd beg to take it off."

"But I want to match with Blue and Cora," she complains to Mom. "Everyone gets a cast but me." Her crocodile tears threaten to reappear.

"The last thing I need is for you to break something."

Sunshine pouts.

Mom appraises her. "I think we have an old splint in the garage—you can wear that if you want."

"Can people sign it? Just like Blue's and Cora's casts?"

"I don't see why not."

"Yes!" she says, jumping up from her seat. Sunshine's back. Her happy atoms zig around her head.

Mom stuffs a paper copy of my X-ray into her bag and pulls out a small slip of paper. "I still can't believe I got a parking ticket last night. You used to be able to park along the pier."

My cast itches. I pick at it, trying to adjust the cotton sock inside.

"I still don't see why you didn't come home last night with us, Cora. Why'd you get a ride with Mr. Mendez?"

I hesitate. "I just wanted to spend time with my new . . . friends."

Mom eyes me skeptically.

"You're all set." The nurse gives the cast a final pat. She turns to Sunshine. "Do you want to pick a prize from the treasure box?"

Mom nods.

Sunshine follows the nurse out. "This is the best day ever!"

Mom gathers her purse and car keys. "I swear, if one more bad thing happens, I'm going back to bed and staying there for a week. I still don't get how you broke it. What happened?"

I take a deep breath. "Patrick and I were at the eclipse and I tripped on something. It was *dark*." I'm the worst liar. "Patrick and I had to measure the water, and, I don't know, I just bumped into him and fell."

Mom waits four seconds. "You broke your hand on the sand?"

Usually, Brain loves a good lie.

Brain says: I do.

"Yeah," I say, a lump in my throat.

Mom's dark eyes bore into mine. Her forehead crinkles. "Okay, Cora. If that's what you say happened." She pauses. "Then I believe you."

My stomach feels shaked and baked. Brain always lied to me, but now, I want the truth. The *new* me always needs the truth.

Mom opens the door to leave.

"Wait." I tug on her sleeve. "That's not how it happened."

We sit down and I tell her everything. When I'm finished, I wait for Mom's reaction. But all she does is tuck her hair behind her ear and purse her lips like she does when she's thinking. She stares at the wallpaper in the doctor's office before saying, "And he believes he went back in time and met his parents?"

I nod, trying to read her eyes.

In eight seconds, she lets out a big breath. "Wow."

"It's a really big wow."

"That's quite a story."

I nod.

"Well, that's a good thing, right?" Mom slips her phone into her purse. "Patrick wanted to meet them, and now he thinks he has."

I nod. *Did he really go back in time?*

"Why not let him be happy?" says Mom.

"Happy *is* good."

She sits up straighter. "But as for you, the train really stopped?"

"I didn't stay to see, but it was slowing down."

"And you were near the tracks?" Mom's eyes narrow, her voice tight.

I look at my feet. "Yes," I whisper-say.

"I can't believe a smart girl like you would do that, Cora. Do you know how dangerous those train tracks are?" She stands.

I swallow—my throat dry with the truth. Honesty sometimes gets you in trouble.

"I'm going to have to talk to your dad about a punishment, but you must promise you'll never do that again."

I fiddle with my cast. "I won't."

Mom hugs me. "I'm serious."

I know.

Sunshine comes in from picking a treasure out of the doctor's treasure chest for me (but really for her). She announces, "I get to be the first one to sign your cast!"

It takes me zero seconds to say, "You got it."

I follow them out the door, down the hall into the lobby.

Sunshine stands in front of the vending machine. "Mommy, I need some money. There are three things I want."

Mom looks over the selections. "Never a dull moment around here."

I stand behind them, gazing at the choices of M&M's, Fudge Stripes cookies, and sour cream and onion chips. "I know where we can get something way better than stale chips in a vending machine," I say.

Sunshine turns, her hands on her hips. "Where?"

The IHOP sign gleams in the sun. Clouds dot the sky but, I know, just beyond the blue lies outer space—dark and mysterious, packed with stars and planets and *time*. Time constantly passing—hours, minutes, seconds, milliseconds—all of it calmly ticks on, keeping track of forever.

Mom parks the car. "Are you sure you're up for Social Skills?"

I nod.

"I called Aunt Janet and Blue—they're here—saving us a table."

"Chocolate chip pancakes!" Sunshine unbuckles her seat belt. She's out the door before I can even fiddle with mine.

I fumble with my buckle; my hand still aches even after taking Advil. "Breakfast with whipped cream sounds good." I hope I sound believable.

Mom comes to my side of the car and helps me with my

seat belt. Then she puts her arm around me. We walk inside like that. Just a regular mom and daughter out to breakfast. *Nothing to see here*, I tell myself, even though my heart feels like it's going to pound out of my chest.

I eye the hostess stand. I take a deep breath and prepare myself to speak, but Mom beats me to it.

"We have a party expecting us," she says to the guy. Then she winks at me. A truce. Maybe we'll put Social Skills on hold.

I walk ahead, but Mom grabs my hand. "Hold on a second. I've been thinking about your wanting to change therapists. It's okay with me if we schedule an appointment with a different doctor."

"It is?" I can really try someone different?

"And I've been thinking about the antianxiety medicine Dr. Rosenthal suggested. Dad and I discussed it and we think it would be good to try, if you want."

"Does that mean you think I'm doing worse?" I ask.

"No! Not at all. Dad and I just see how hard you're trying, and we think some medicine may make things easier for you," Mom says.

"Okay," I say. "Maybe."

"Dad and I are on the same page now."

"You are?" After weeks of them fighting, it feels impossible.

"We just want you to be happy, okay?" Mom squeezes my hand.

"I want to be happy too."

She points to my chest. "We named you Cora because it

means heart. Even as a baby we could see you had a sensitive one. This is where you need to live." She points again to my chest. "Here." She points to my head. "Not here."

Not with Brain.

I put my hand over my heart. Knowing I have choices makes my stomach feel less squished. I won't have to quiet Brain all by myself.

Aunt Janet and Blue wave at us from across the restaurant. Sunshine's already with them in the booth.

I follow Mom to the table.

"Cora, you have a cast just like mine!" Blue says. Our casts glow in twin neon.

"I wanted us to match."

He laughs, his eyes bright. "Now we both have zombie arms!" He karate chops the air.

"Zombie powers unite," I say. It feels good to be forgiven.

The waiter places water and menus on the table.

Aunt Janet says, "We're expecting two more."

Two more?

Mom scans the restaurant. "There they are." She points to the hostess stand.

I turn.

Dad and Uncle Richie come toward us. Dad fast, Richie slow.

"Daddy!" yells Sunshine. She bolts down the aisle and jumps into his arms. "Daddy, can I get a cast, *please*?"

Mom laughs and rolls her eyes. "Typical."

"How's your hand?" asks Aunt Janet as she leans closer to me. "What happened? I need all the juicy details."

Mom scoffs. "Oh, it's a juicy story, all right. A story that almost ended with much worse than a broken hand." She gives me the side-eye.

Aunt Janet winks at me. "I can't wait to hear."

Dad slides next to me in the booth and examines my cast. "Looks like they did a good job patching you up."

"Just like new," I say. I like having Dad on my side again.

Uncle Richie stands awkwardly next to us, his thigh almost touching our table. I can feel how uncomfortable he is.

Dad looks at his watch. "Rich has forty-five minutes before he's expected back at the center."

He nods, so alone.

"Well, sit down," Mom says to him. "This is a family brunch, isn't it?"

Uncle Richie scans the table.

Dad slides out of the booth and stands.

I take a deep breath. If Dad can forgive him, so can I. "You can sit next to me," I say. I feel my face only get a teeny-tiny bit hot.

Mom pats his hand. "It's about time we fixed this."

My uncle clears his throat but doesn't sit. "Thank you for inviting me." His face still reddens.

"Thank you for being here," I say, louder than a whisper.

"I just want to say one thing. I want to say how sorry I am for everything in the past—for the money, and the car, and for leaving Cora when I should've been there."

I can't read Mom's expression, but she nods slightly.

He grabs the edge of the table like it's helping to hold him up. "I can't predict the future, but my goal is to remain sober.

It's hard, but I'm happier when I'm healthy—I'm going to do my best to stay that way."

Mom looks Uncle Richie right in the eyes. "Thank you for apologizing. I think I'm ready to leave it in the past."

A slow smile spreads across Uncle Richie's face. He doesn't smile much, but when he does, man is it worth it, like sunlight coming out from behind the clouds.

Everyone at our table smiles back.

Sunshine whispers to me, "I like him."

Finally, Uncle Richie sits.

Dad sits next to him and puts his arm around his brother. They sit side by side, just like peas and carrots. Just like toast and jam.

Brain says: Like Taco Tuesday.

The waiter comes over and looks at me first.

"Cool green cast. Can I take your order, miss?" The table falls quiet. My heart pounds.

Sunshine says, "She'll have—"

"I got it," I interrupt.

Sunshine's mouth falls open in surprise.

I take a deep breath and look the waiter right in the eyes. "I'll have French toast with strawberries, please."

He nods and writes it down.

I add, "With extra whipped cream."

I text Minny: Next time you visit, let's go to IHOP.

CHAPTER 43

Four Weeks Later: 14 Minutes Until The Unattainable Find

*P*atrick and I ride our bikes past the jetty. His burned hair has mostly grown back. Queen Bea made him cut it short after the lunar eclipse. Even now, when I see him, I almost laugh.

"She made me lose all my power!" he says, popping a wheelie. "I *need* my hair."

"You've still got it," I say. "Plus, it's growing back."

He jumps the curb with his bike he really named Time Machine Two.

I follow him.

He still believes he traveled through time and met his mom and dad, and we've all decided to let him believe it. "I came back, didn't I? That shows you how much I like it here!"

His new project is Time Travel, the Sequel. Of course, I'm still his second. Queen Bea says he's not allowed near trains or car batteries. But Patrick's over that. He has a new idea, time travel with wind turbines.

We turn right and head up the beach trail. The palm trees sway in the breeze. The sun burns bright and beautiful in the sky. Our bikes thump over the railroad tracks as we pass the aloe vera plants and oleander bushes. The dirt path takes us farther, until we reach the narrow steps, so clear to me now I can't believe I never saw them before.

We park our bikes a little off the beach trail and lock them together with the others. Patrick has taped the newly scorched Neil Armstrong figure to his flowered basket.

"Hellooo!" Patrick waves to someone up on the hill. I shade my eyes. Ando's house sits in the distance.

"Come on," I say. I carry Ruva up the steps. And Patrick carries his new metal detector from Queen Bea.

I've decided that most people are nothing like I expect. Time will tell me who they are.

We open the gate.

Ando stands in his backyard, impatient. "Dude, what took you guys so long?"

Humberto stands next to him, acting much nicer than he did the night of our time travel. I convinced Patrick to let him hang out with us. Everyone deserves a second chance. I'm trying to listen more with my heart.

Patrick responds, "Queen Bea wouldn't let me leave." She has a tighter grip on him since the lunar eclipse.

Ando waves his phone. "You've got to see this new app. It measures wind velocity. All you've got to do is attach the gauge here." He points to the port on his phone and holds up a cord with a little paddle at the end. "My dad uses it at surf camp."

Ando, Patrick, and Humberto sit on the bench to examine it. Ando's now Patrick's third-in-command, which is just fine with me.

I look at my watch, a gift from Dad after I broke my hand. "For luck," he said. Its face is embedded in a tiny padlock. The second hand ticks happily around.

"Come on, guys," I say. "Let's get to down to Cat's Cove." I still haven't given up on The Unattainable Find.

Patrick grabs his metal detector. The boys follow me down the path and get on their bikes. We bounce over potholes and zip around people, a pack of explorers.

A pack of friends, brain.

The sun feels nice on my face and arms, my hoodie tied around my waist. We ditch our bikes at the top of PCH and dash down the path.

Humberto trips at the bottom.

We all laugh. So does he.

Cat's Cove isn't empty. There are three other kids here.

That's okay.

My phone dings. I pull it out of my pocket.

Minny texts: Im cominggg 2 visit over Thanks-giving Break!!!!!!

I text: NOOOOO !!!!!!! ☺ ☺ ☺ ☺

Minny texts: YESSSS. :0 :0 :0 :0 :0 we'll find the cat's treasure tgthr

I text: ALL of us

Patrick, Ando, and Humberto wrestle in the sand. Minny's going to die when she sees who I hang out with now.

I put my phone away and slap on my headphones. I flip Ruva's switch.

Beep. Beep. Beep.

A storm passed through La Quinta Beach this weekend, so the waves are a little stronger than usual. The muffled sounds of Patrick, Ando, and Humberto's wrestle mania evaporate. In eight seconds, I'm focused. I wave the paddle over the sand and pebbles and pretty rocks, scrubbed clean by the current, washed ashore.

I take a step into the water and another, deeper than usual, as I follow a trail of rocks gleaming in and out of the murk. Pebbles and seaweed swirl around my shins, along with the stirred-up sludge from the storm.

"Ouch." I stub my toe and reach for a jagged rock in my path when something glints in the dark water. Something gold.

I shiver. Clouds cover the sun; a cool breeze ripples over the cove.

The treasure?

I swing Ruva's paddle over the water. It beeps, slow at first, then faster and faster. The waves rush in. The glint—gold and roundish. A coin?

The tide pulls out, the current shifts everything and the glint disappears.

I rip off my headphones and grab the sifter on my belt. "Guys!" I yell, trying to keep my eyes on the treasure. "I found something! Come here, quick!"

I turn. But they're gone.

"Cora!" Patrick yells.

I look up.

They're on PCH. On the bridge.

"Hurry! The trolley's running again! We're going to the pier!"

I shake my head. My feet itch to follow the gold.

"Cora!" yells Ando.

"Cora!" yells Humberto.

My heart bumps.

"We're holding it for you!" Patrick waves his arms frantically. "We need our second!"

I swallow. Milliseconds and seconds whoosh around my head, making me dizzy.

Now I understand Dad. It isn't about the treasure. It's about time. Time with people you care about.

The wave rolls back in, scattering sticks and mud over the shoreline—the glint now gone. Lost.

I grab Ruva and hear a loud meow. I turn. A black cat sits on top of a boulder, staring down at me. *Catherine Van Larr?*

"I see you, Cat! I see it all!"

It meows again and slinks through the aloe vera plants, disappearing behind the boulders.

"Cora!" yells Patrick, more urgent.

"I'm coming!" I've waited this long to find the treasure; I can wait a little longer.

I bolt up the path and jump inside the trolley, just as it pulls away from the curb.

"You made it!" Patrick gives me a high five and points to a

seat between himself and Ando. Humberto squishes in next to Patrick. The trolley's packed. La Quinta Beach is already feeling the crush of November holiday crowds. Early Christmas music plays over the speakers.

Humberto says, "You almost missed it."

"I wouldn't let the driver leave." Ando flexes his muscles.

Patrick and Humberto laugh; their long arms stretch over me to punch him.

You missed the treasure, brain says.

I slightly shake my head.

No.

Eight minutes *can* change your life, but it takes me far less time to realize. Seconds, even.

The treasure is here. I'm in it, now.

The Unattainable Find.

The nicest thing about the rain is that it
always stops. Eventually.
—A. A. Milne

Dear Reader,

I'm not a psychologist, a doctor, or a mental health professional. I'm not an expert in, well, anything, really.

But I am a person. I'm certain I'm alive.

Maybe that's what I'm an expert in—being alive. And so are you. Being alive means that there's a good chance we'll struggle with our mental health at some point. We might struggle with it every day. That's okay. No one is always happy. Sadness and anxiety are a normal part of being human, so that means we need to have more discussions about our brains.

In the United States, approximately 4.4 million children, ages three to seventeen years, have been diagnosed with anxiety. Approximately 1.9 million children, ages three to seventeen years, have been diagnosed with depression.[1] That's a lot of children who are feeling worried, scared, and overwhelmed.

---

1. Reem M. Ghandour, DrPH, MPA, Laura J. Sherman, PhD, Catherine J. Vladutiu, PhD, MPH, Sean E. Lynch, PhD, LCSW, Rebecca H. Bitsko, PhD, Stephen J Blumberg, PhD, "Prevalence and Treatment of Depression, Anxiety, and Conduct Problems in US Children," *The Journal of Pediatrics*, 2018. Published online before print October 12, 2018.

Anxiety and depression lie to you and sometimes it's difficult to tell the lies from the truth.

LIES OF ANXIETY AND DEPRESSION

1. Depression and anxiety aren't real. I'm just too sensitive.
2. Being anxious and depressed is my personality.
3. It would feel weird to ask for help or see a counselor.
4. I have a great life. I have no excuse to be depressed or anxious.
5. I have no friends. No one understands me.

TRUTHS THAT I KNOW

1. You're worthy of love and friendship.
2. You're not alone.
3. You haven't done anything wrong.
4. You can get support that will help you feel better.
5. You're a good person.

If you feel like you may be suffering from anxiety, depression, or another mental health concern, please tell someone. Talk to your parents, a trusted adult, a teacher, a doctor, or a school counselor. Tell them how you're feeling. It's good to talk about it. It's good to ask for help. You're going to be okay.

Please know that *I know* you deserve to be happy, just like Cora.

Sincerely,
Jen White

If you or someone you love is in crisis, please call:

Lifeline 1-800-273-TALK

www.suicidepreventionlifeline.org

To find out more about mental health statistics, please visit www.cdc.gov/childrensmentalhealth/data.html.

ACKNOWLEDGMENTS

Thank you to my agent, Charlotte Sheedy, forever my champion. Thank you to my editor, Joy Peskin, for her wise and careful insight.

Thank you to assistant editor Elizabeth Lee. Thank you for the beautiful cover, created by artist Jenna Stempel-Lobell and designer Cassie Gonzales.

Thank you to Diane Hoffman LPC-S, who gave me great understanding and feedback. Any mistakes in this book are completely my own.

Thank you to N. Griffin, Autumn McAlpin, Amy Osmond Cook, Natalie Hill, and Minette Daland, who offer cheer, laughter, and minutes upon minutes of important conversation.

Thank you to Teri Bailey Black, Aubrey Hartman, Melanie Jacobson, Brittany Larsen, and Tiffany Odekirk, for always providing encouragement and a writer's ear.

Thank you to Kim and Terresa, who are with me in everything I write.

Thank you to my twelve-year-old nieces and nephews, Maria, Sam, Amber, Jaxon, Brody, and Shaunalia, who are thoughtful book lovers and a loyal fan club.

A huge thanks to my family for their love as well as physical and mental space to write. Thank you to Spencer, Grace, Sophie, Lucy, and Lola. Thank you to Adam.

And finally, thank you to my readers. Without you, I'd be talking to myself.